This book is to be returned on or before
the last date stamped below.

Library Services
Victoria Buildings
Queen Street
Falkirk
FK2 7AF

221
FUR

ANE FOR A'

Falkirk Council

For my grandchildren,
Coral, Joseph and Eve.
M.F.

For Sue Phipps, timegiver.
C.D.

DREAMERS OF DREAMS

Text copyright © 2001 by Monica Furlong
Ilustrations copyright © 2001 by Cherry Denman

First published in Great Britain in 2001

The right of Monica Furlong to be identified as the Author of the Work has been asserted by her in accordance with the
Copyright, Designs and Patents Act 1988.

10 9 8 7 6 5 4 3 2 1

British Library Cataloguing in Publication Data
A record for this book is available from the British Library

ISBN 0 340 78548 9

Printed and bound in Spain by Imago

Hodder & Stoughton
A Division of Hodder Headline Ltd
338 Euston Road
London NW1 3BH

DREAMERS OF DREAMS

TALES OF THE OLD TESTAMENT

TOLD BY
MONICA FURLONG

ILLUSTRATED BY
CHERRY DENMAN

Hodder & Stoughton
A MEMBER OF THE HODDER HEADLINE GROUP

CONTENTS

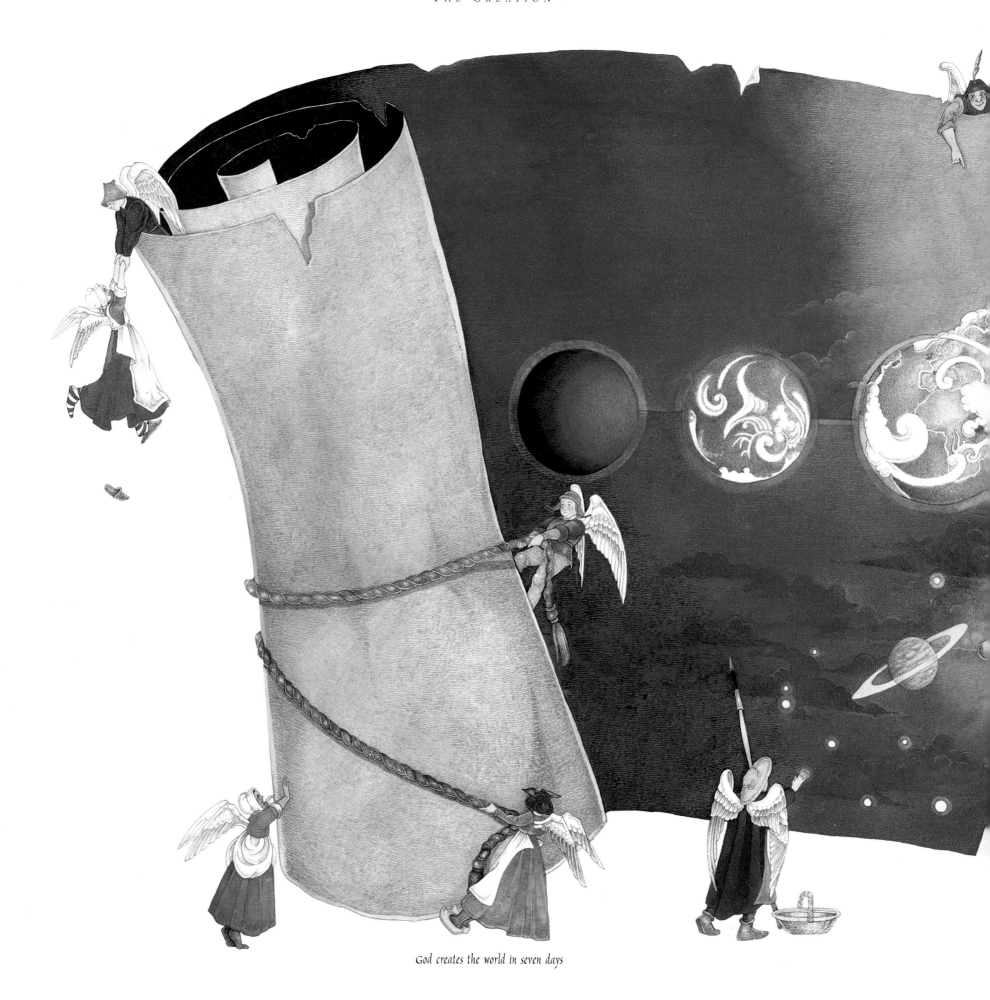

God creates the world in seven days

Genesis 1-2

THE CREATION

In the beginning, the very beginning of everything, there was almost nothing. There was water, and there was darkness, but nothing else. There was no sun, no moon, no land, no animals, no trees, no people. And because there was almost nothing there, nothing ever happened. Over the water, however, moved the Power, the Energy, the mysterious presence that human beings later came to call God, the Imagination which would transform everything. So one day something did happen. God started to create the world, and, like an artist, he worked and worked away at his creation until it was just the way he wanted it, and eventually he decided it was complete.

First of all, he imagined light. 'Let there be light,' he said, and there was light. Think what that must have been like – total darkness and then, suddenly, light! He gave this new invention a name, 'Day', and since he wanted it to alternate with darkness, he gave the darkness a name too, 'Night'. This huge labour took a whole day of his time.

On the second day God first imagined, and then made, 'Heaven', the fixed point around which he was going to arrange the rest of his creation. This was a stupendous effort.

On the third day God gathered up the waters here and there so that they no longer covered everything. Dry land began to appear. God called the dry land 'Earth', and the waters he called 'Sea'. He looked at all he had done so far and, like anyone who makes something, felt pleased. He saw that he had made something beautiful. And he was inspired to imagine new, wonderful things to add to his creation, and to bring them into being. He imagined grass and flowers, trees and plants, seeds that would grow into fruit, and soon all of these existed. All this was the work of the third day.

Then he placed great lights in the heavens, the sun to bring light to the earth and the moon to give gentler beams at night. The sun and the moon between them would divide day from night, season from season, and year from year. He set stars in the sky to bring light upon the earth in the darkness of the night. The effect of it all was very beautiful, and once again God felt joy in the glory of what he had created.

On the fifth day God spoke to the waters and commanded living creatures into being – every sort of fish and sea creature you can think of. And among these he invented the marvel of the great whale. He imagined birds, and straight away birds began to fly in the sky above the earth. He told the fish and the whales and the birds to breed and to bring many more fish and whales and birds into being. Then, out of his boundless imagination, God invented animals – dinosaurs, the great beasts of the jungle, snakes and insects, horses and cattle, every sort of animal you can think of, and some that you can't. These, too, he commanded to breed and to fill the earth with their kind.

Then, in a final great burst of energy, he imagined human beings, men and women, and said that of all the creatures he had made these were the ones most like himself, the most imaginative, the most intelligent, the most inventive. Humans, he said, were to be in charge of this world he had created. Out of his love for them he blessed them, and commanded them to breed and fill his earth with people, as he had commanded the fish and the birds and the animals. He told them that the plants

which he had created for them would give them abundant food, and that there would be enough food for all the living creatures he had made.

God had spent six days making his world, and he looked at the result with pleasure because he saw that what he had imagined was very good.

On the seventh day, exhausted by his work, he rested, and he said that in future the seventh day of the week would always be a special day because that was the day on which he had rested from his work, and therefore it was a day on which his creatures should rest, too.

Until this time there had been no rain upon the earth. But then God sent clouds and rain which watered the whole earth so that plants could grow. And that was how the world came into being.

Adam and Eve enjoy the
Garden of Eden

Genesis 2-4

The snake tempts Eve

THE GARDEN OF EDEN

Adam and Eve are driven
from the garden

Cain kills his brother Abel

Cain is marked by God

THE GARDEN OF EDEN

There is another, slightly different, story about how God created men and women. In this version, God made the man first. He took clay from the ground, and, like a potter or a sculptor, he moulded it into the shape of a man, and then he breathed into the nostrils and the model became alive, a living man. As a home for this man, God made a glorious garden in a place called Eden, and he filled it with fine fruit-bearing trees and plants that were good for food. In the middle of the garden he planted two special trees – one that he called the Tree of Life, and one that he called the Tree of the Knowledge of Good and Evil. Through the garden flowed a great river, which watered the plants in the Garden of Eden.

When the work of making the Garden of Eden was complete, God placed the man there to enjoy it and take care of it. God said to the man, 'You may eat whatever food you like from this garden – have as much as you wish – with one exception. You must not eat from the Tree of the Knowledge of Good and Evil, the one set in the middle of the garden, because if you do, it will kill you.'

God called the man 'Adam', which means 'a man'. In turn he brought each of the animals and birds and creatures that he had made to Adam so that he could give them names, saying that whatever Adam chose to call them, that would be their name.

God was troubled, however, that Adam, unlike all the animals, had no mate. So he put him into a deep sleep, and as he slept he took a rib from his side and made it into a woman. And then he healed the wound that he had made in Adam's side. When Adam woke up, God brought the woman that he had made and showed her to Adam. Adam was delighted with her, and said that, because she had come from his side, she would always be very special to him. She was bone of his bone and flesh of his flesh, in fact, part of himself, and therefore more important to him than anyone else. Adam called this new being 'Woman'. Adam and the Woman were very happy together. They walked without clothes in the beautiful garden and did not find it at all embarrassing or shameful.

There were many animals and other creatures living in the Garden of Eden, but the cleverest of them all was the snake. The snake was fascinated by the Tree of the Knowledge of Good and Evil and the fact that God had told Adam not to eat of its fruit. (Adam had told the Woman about this.) The snake was full of curiosity about what would happen if one of them did eat the fruit.

Cunningly, the snake said to the Woman, 'Is it not the case that you are allowed to eat fruit from any tree in the garden if you want to?'

'That's not quite right,' said the Woman innocently. 'God said that we may eat the fruit of any tree we like, with one exception. We may not eat the fruit of the tree in the middle of the garden, the one he calls the Tree of the Knowledge of Good and Evil. God says that if we eat of it, or even touch it, we may die.'

'Well, that's nonsense,' said the snake. 'I can promise you that you won't die. God does not want you to eat from that tree because if you do you will know too much. You will be as wise as gods and you won't do what God tells you to do any more. This is his way of making you obey him.'

Because of this conversation, the Woman became

fascinated by the tree. She went and looked at it, and thought how beautiful it was, and how delicious the fruit looked.

She picked one of the fruit and ate it, and then she gave another to Adam, and he ate too.

Immediately, everything began to change. The simple happiness they had enjoyed together in the Garden of Eden was spoiled. Instead of walking about naked together and feeling completely happy, they felt awkward and embarrassed. They were so embarrassed that they picked fig leaves, sewed them together and made them into a sort of clothing.

God liked to walk in the garden in the cool of the day, and as he had often done before, he called to Adam and Eve to come and be with him so that he might enjoy their company. Instead of running to meet him joyfully, however, as they usually did, they hid themselves among the trees.

God called, 'Where are you?'

Emerging shamefacedly from the trees, Adam replied, 'I heard your voice in the garden and I felt afraid because I was naked. So I went and hid myself.'

God said sternly, 'Who told you that you were naked? You never noticed it before. Have you eaten of the tree from which I told you not to eat?'

Like a sneak, Adam decided to blame the Woman. He mumbled, 'Well, yes. It was not really my fault. The Woman gave me the forbidden fruit, and I ate it.'

So God turned to the Woman and said, 'What have you done?'

Just like Adam, the Woman blamed someone else. 'The serpent told me to eat the fruit, so I did.'

God called upon the snake and cursed it, and said that, for ever after, it would be the lowest of all creatures for having spoiled God's great creation. Then God turned again to the Woman and told her that the gentleness and innocence of his plan for men and women had been spoiled and now everything was going to be different. As a woman she would bear children, but it would be painful, and bringing them up would be hard.

Now her husband would take charge of her and control her, whether she liked it or not.

To Adam, God said that because he had been so weak and done exactly what the Woman had tempted him to do, though he knew it was wrong, his life too would be a hard one. Instead of the ease and contentment of Eden, he would have to toil from morning till night to grow the food he and his family needed, and it would always be a struggle. The old happiness, when he and the Woman had lived peacefully with the animals and had not needed to do any work, had gone for ever.

God understood that Adam and the Woman could no longer live without clothes, and he made them coats of skins. But he had not finished with them yet. He drove them eastwards out of Eden, out of the lovely garden that he had made specially for them, and he placed cherubim, angels with flaming swords, at the entrance to the garden, so that never again would they be able to get back inside and make their way to the Tree of Life.

The Woman was pregnant, the first woman ever to be so, and Adam called her Eve, the mother of all living people, because everyone else would be descended from her. Eve had twin boys, whom she called Cain and Abel. Adam was a farmer now, and Abel grew up to look after the sheep and Cain to grow crops. Cain had a bitter and quarrelsome disposition, and one day when he and Abel were out in the fields together Cain picked a quarrel, and in a fit of rage killed Abel.

God summoned Cain and said to him, 'Where is Abel, your brother?'

And Cain replied rudely, 'I have no idea. I am not his keeper.'

God said, 'Cain, what have you done? The blood of the brother that you have killed cries out to me from the ground where he lies. Never again will the ground yield food for you – you have polluted it. Now you will wander the earth, unloved and unwanted.'

Because God felt sorry for Eve he gave her another son, called Seth, and from his many descendants was born a man called Noah.

NOAH

Noah fills his ark with animals

The ark is safely afloat as the rains begin

The dove returns with an olive branch

Genesis 6-9

The animals return to dry land

Noah in his tent after a night enjoying his wine

NOAH

Many years after Adam and Eve had lived and died, their descendant Noah was born. By this time there were lots of people on earth, all of them descendants of Adam and Eve, and there were also giants, but I don't know from whom they were descended.

God had begun to be very disappointed in his creation because he saw that men and women, whom he had meant to be the crown of his work, did wicked things that hurt other people, and sometimes he wished that he had never thought of making them. The whole world that he had made, he noticed, seemed to be full of violence, and men were proud of this.

Finally, things got so bad that God decided on the drastic step of doing away with his creation, both human beings and the whole animal creation, because he felt his great work was a failure. The only thing that made him hesitate was Noah. Noah truly loved God and was a man of great goodness, and God could not bear to destroy him. Noah by this time had three sons, Shem, Ham and Japheth.

God spoke to Noah and told him how horrified he was at the violence that was now common among men, and how he could not bear it to continue. He was going to destroy the earth, he said. But first he wanted Noah to build an ark, as he called it, that is to say a large ship, of gopher wood, with decks at different levels, and with many cabins inside it. He was to cover it carefully with pitch inside and out, so that the water could not get in. God was very specific about the size of the ship, and about its length and width, and he said that the ark must have a window, and a big door set in the side.

Noah naturally asked what all this was for, and God replied that there was going to be a tremendous flood, which would drown all the people and all the animals on earth. But as for Noah, God made a promise that he and his whole family, his wife, his sons and his sons' wives, would all come out of the flood safely. Before the flood came, however, God asked Noah and his family to perform a very difficult task. They had to take two of every sort of animal, bird, insect and serpent, male and female, and to lead or carry them on to the ark, two at a time, so that they would not drown in the flood. This, of course, would also mean taking a lot of food on board to feed such a large family of people and animals. Obediently, Noah and his family did exactly what God told them to do.

God told Noah that in seven days' time the great flood would start, but to have no fear, since because of his goodness he would be safe. When the waters came Noah and his family, and all the animals who were going to be saved, must be safely aboard. It would rain, God said, for forty days and forty nights, and everyone and everything that God had previously created would be drowned or washed away, except for Noah and his cargo.

So, as the rain began, Noah and his family joined the animals on the ark, and God shut them inside. To begin with, the ark stood, propped up, on dry land, but as the rain became heavier and the water began to rise, the ark started to float. It sailed out upon the waters, and everywhere, as far as Noah and his family could see, there was nothing but water. Even the highest hills and mountains disappeared under the waves. And, of course, every living thing was submerged, not only people and animals, but all the crops, plants and trees. Every living creature except those on the ark was drowned. Alone in the whole world, Noah and his family floated out across the great sheet of water.

Eventually God caused the rain to stop and a wind to blow, which helped disperse the deep waters, though even then there was water everywhere. The ark, meanwhile, had come to rest on what was once a mountain, Mount Ararat. Noah noticed that gradually, day by day, the waters were going down. In the tenth month after the rain started he observed that he could see the tops of the mountains sticking out above the water. So he opened the window and sent out a raven, knowing that if the bird could find a resting place for his feet, he would not return. But he did return. Noah waited another seven days before sending out a little dove, and she came back bearing a twig of olive in her mouth, which showed Noah that the flood was abating fast, and that some trees had survived. Seven days later he sent her out once more, and this time she did not come back, so he guessed that that meant she had found herself a place to build a nest. So he took the protective covering off the ark, and looked out, and he could see that the ground around the ark was already beginning to dry up.

Eventually the ground was more or less dry, and God told Noah to leave the ark and let all the creatures he had saved go out into the hills and forests and plains and breed once more, so that the earth would be full of creatures again.

In gratitude for his survival, Noah built an altar and made a sacrifice to God, and God took pleasure in this and said to himself that he would never again destroy the people and animals of the earth. God made a promise to himself that as long as the earth continued to exist, season would follow season, seed-time would be followed by harvest, there would be cold and heat, winter and summer, night and day. These would be the fixed points of human life. Because of the faithfulness and goodness of Noah, he was prepared to

preserve his creation whatever happened.

So he said to Noah, 'I give my blessing to you and to all your family.' He said, as he had previously said to Adam and Eve, 'Be fruitful, have many children, go out and take care of my creation. The animals and birds and fishes will be subject to you, and they, together with the plants of the earth, may be your food, but I require you to treat their lives with care, and to treat the lives of each other with care. I will hold any man responsible if he takes the life of another man, since all human beings are made in my own image.'

Then God blessed Noah and his children again, and again told them to have many children and to care for the earth. Then he said, 'I am going to make a covenant, that is, an agreement, with you and with your descendants, and with all the creatures that came out of the ark and their descendants. Never again will I set out to destroy my creation. This is my solemn promise to you and to all those who will live upon the earth in the future. I shall create a sign which will always remind you of my promise. The sign is the rainbow. When you see the rainbow among the rain clouds you will be reminded of the lasting agreement I have made with all the living creatures of the earth.'

So the terrible flood was a new beginning for creation, and the start of a closer relationship between God and those who survived it. All this really depended on the faithfulness and goodness of Noah, who alone gave God trust in human beings.

Even Noah did not always behave perfectly, however. One night he got very drunk on some delicious wine from his own vineyard. His sons could hear him snoring away in his tent, and had to go in and cover him up to stop him catching cold.

He lived to a great old age, as did his sons Shem, Ham and Japheth. The sons divided up all the lands of the earth between them, and gradually their families spread and spread.

THE TOWER OF BABEL

Genesis 11-19

Building the Tower of Babel

Sarah challenges Hagar

The strangers tell Abraham that Sarah will bear a child

The fall of Sodom and Gomorrah

The angel tells Hagar that
she will bear a son

Abraham prepares to sacrifice
Isaac

Isaac meets Rebekah
at the well

Genesis 19-24

THE TOWER OF BABEL

In those very early days of the human race, everyone spoke the same language, so that even if you travelled long distances it was easy to talk to other people. Some of the descendants of Shem travelled to the land of Shinar, and there they had what they thought was a wonderful idea. They had learned how to make bricks, and also mortar to stick together the bricks, which they made out of wet clay. So they had the very ambitious idea of building first of all a huge city, and then, in the middle of it, a gigantic tower, a tower so high that it would reach up to heaven itself. (They did this because they thought it would make them famous.) So they built and built and built, and soon had the highest tower that anyone on earth had ever seen, so that it did make them famous.

God watched them building this tower and he felt uneasy. He thought that they were too proud, that they were getting above themselves, and that if they managed to build a tower that reached up to heaven there was no knowing what they would do next. So he hit on the idea of muddling up the language they used, in such a way that different people spoke different languages and found it hard to understand one another, and in the end this made it so difficult to finish the tower that the builders gave up in disgust. And since then, people in different countries have always found it difficult to understand one another.

GOD'S SERVANT ABRAHAM

From time to time God chose someone to help him fulfil his plan for humankind – it was usually, though not always, someone good. The first of such people that he chose was a man called Abram (God later called him Abraham, but we shall come to that) who lived in a place called Ur. Abram and his wife Sarai lived in tents, as many people did in those days and some still do today, and they kept flocks of sheep to provide them with food and clothing. To their grief they had no children.

God said to Abram, 'I want you to leave Ur and your father and mother, and travel to a land that I will show you. I have chosen you to be the father of a great nation, and I shall bless you and you will be famous. I shall support you in this great task, and through you every family on earth will be blessed.'

So Abram, who was a good and devout man, set out as God had told him to, and he took with him his wife Sarai and his nephew Lot, and all his camels and sheep and oxen and donkeys, and many friends and servants, and they all set off for Canaan. When they got to Canaan, God said to Abram, 'This is the country which I mean to give you.'

Abram and Lot had so many flocks and herds between them that the land could not provide pasture for all of them, and their herdsmen started quarrelling about where their animals were allowed to graze.

Abram said to Lot, 'Look here, we are of one family, are we not, and we must not quarrel. We have a huge country in front of us. If you wish to take the left-hand side of the country for your cattle then you are welcome to do so, and I will take the right-hand side. Or if you prefer the right-hand side, I am content to take the left-hand side. It is for you to choose.'

Lot chose the fertile plain of Jordan, so he took his flocks and settled there. And Abram settled in Canaan.

'Look around you,' God said to Abram.

'Everything you can see I give to you and to your descendants. And you will have many, many descendants. Get up, and walk over this land and look at it, for it is now yours.'

So Abram walked across his land, and settled in Hebron and built an altar to God there. Yet he was puzzled that God talked of the many children, and children's children, that he was to have, since his wife Sarai had not had even one child. What could it mean? Finally, Sarai, who grieved that she had not had a child and knew how much Abram wanted children, made a very loving offer to Abram. Sarai had a bondwoman, a sort of slave, an Egyptian girl called Hagar. Sarai suggested, as was a custom of the time, that Abram might take Hagar as a second wife so that he could have children by her and his name would not die out.

Hagar did conceive a child by Abram, and immediately began to feel very contemptuous and superior to her mistress Sarai, who had not been able to have a child.

Then Sarai went to Abram and poured out her distress and anger about Hagar's unkindness, and Abram took her side and said that she was Hagar's mistress and must do as she wished. Sarai was so angry that Hagar became frightened and ran away. As she rested at a fountain in the wilderness, an angel came to her and told her to return to Sarai and do as she told her. The angel said that she, Hagar, would bear a son and must give him the name Ishmael.

God told Abram that he would now be called Abraham, instead of Abram – it meant 'the father of many nations'. And Sarai would be called Sarah, which meant 'mother of nations'. Abram or Abraham found this hard to believe, since Sarah still had no children. When God told him that Sarah would bear a child, Abraham tried not to let God see his disbelief – both he and his wife were too old to have a child by now. But God insisted that they would, and that the child's name would be Isaac, and that both Isaac and

Ishmael would be the ancestors of princes.

One day Abraham was sitting at the door of his tent in the heat of the day when he saw three strangers approaching. He stood up and bowed, and immediately offered them the courtesies of the desert.

He told Sarah to hurry and bake cakes of bread, and he himself killed a calf and ordered a servant to prepare it with butter and milk.

The three visitors ate their meal in the shade of the tree, and then they asked Abraham where Sarah was. With the modesty of the desert women Sarah had remained out of sight, and Abraham replied, 'In the tent.' And one of the men said, 'Tell her that she will bear a child.'

Sarah was listening to this conversation from inside the tent, and she laughed grimly to herself. 'Does he really think I am going to have a child at my age? The man's a fool.'

Abraham heard Sarah laugh in the tent, but even as he did so, God put it into Abraham's mind that if God willed it, Sarah could still bear a child, and he went in and told Sarah this and rebuked her for laughing. Sarah was frightened and denied that she had laughed, but Abraham said, 'I heard you.'

Then the three strangers set off, and Abraham went with them to show them the way. God was delighted with Abraham, with his goodness and faithfulness and the excellent way he cared for his family and his household. He confided to him his plan to destroy the city of Sodom, where the people flouted God's commandments and behaved with violence and cruelty and sexual corruption. Abraham was dismayed and suggested that there must be some righteous people there, perhaps fifty, perhaps forty-five, perhaps forty, or thirty, or twenty, or even only ten. Could not God spare the city because of the goodness of ten righteous men? But God could not find even ten.

As it happened, Lot and his family were living in Sodom, and the angel of God warned them to flee before God destroyed the city. Abraham, watching from far away, saw the smoke of fire billowing up into the sky from Sodom and Gomorrah, the cities of the plain, as God destroyed them. It was a terrible thing to see.

Just as God had said he would, he caused Sarah to conceive, to her amazement and delight and to the joy of Abraham. 'Who could have imagined,' she said, 'that one day old Sarah would suckle a baby?' And she laughed again, but this time with happiness.

She and Abraham called their son Isaac, as God had told them to do, and they circumcised him on the eighth day, as was the custom. On the day that Isaac was weaned they gave a great feast, and invited friends and neighbours. The feast was spoiled for Sarah, however, by the sight of Ishmael, Hagar's son, mocking her and the baby, and she went furiously to Abraham and demanded that Hagar and Ishmael should be sent away.

Abraham grieved, because he loved Ishmael and was proud of him. God, however, said to him, 'Don't grieve. Do as Sarah has said, and send Hagar away. Through Isaac shall a great nation arise. But because Ishmael is your son and I have chosen you, he too shall become the father of a nation.'

So early next day Abraham gave Hagar food and a bottle of water, and sent her and Ishmael out into the desert of Beersheba. And when they had drunk all the water, Hagar despaired. She put Ishmael in some shade to sleep and moved away from him, thinking how she could not bear to watch her child die of hunger and thirst. She sat down some distance away and wept her heart out because she could still hear Ishmael crying.

God too heard Ishmael's cries, and he sent an angel to Hagar to tell her that all would be well, that her son would survive and become a great man, and that she should go to him and take him by the hand. She obeyed, and as she did so she noticed a well in the desert and went to it, and filled her water bottle and gave it to Ishmael. Ishmael was to grow up in the desert and become a very skilled archer, and

eventually to marry an Egyptian woman and have many descendants.

ISAAC THE SACRIFICE

One day, God told Abraham to take his son Isaac and set off with him on an expedition to a mountain called Moriah. The terrible thing that God asked of Abraham was, when he got there, to offer his beloved son Isaac as a sacrifice on the mountain. Abraham always obeyed God, so he got up at dawn and saddled his ass, and set off with Isaac and two menservants. On the way he cut wood, to be ready for the sacrificial fire, and rode to Moriah with a heavy heart. The journey took three days. When they could see the mountain he told the two servants to wait behind with the ass, and he and Isaac would go on to the mountain to worship God.

When they got there he gave Isaac the wood to carry, and he himself carried the knife and the fire, and they went on to the place of sacrifice. And Isaac said, 'Father, I see the wood and the fire, but where is the sacrifice?'

And Abraham, his heart breaking, said, 'My son, God will provide a sacrifice.'

When they got to the place of sacrifice, Abraham built an altar and arranged the wood, and bound his terrified son and laid him upon the altar. But as Abraham took up the knife to kill Isaac, an angel called to him, 'Abraham! Abraham!'

And Abraham replied, 'Here am I.'

The angel said, 'Do not kill the boy. You have shown your absolute obedience to God in offering him what you loved most in the world.'

Then Abraham noticed a ram, caught by its horns in the thicket, and he took it and offered it instead of Isaac, as a burnt offering to God. And Isaac was saved.

Isaac grew up. His mother Sarah died, which caused great grief to him and Abraham. Abraham knew that it was time for Isaac to marry, and he took it into his head that he should not marry a Canaanite woman, but a woman of his own people of Ur. Abraham was not strong enough to make such a long journey himself, but he commanded a servant to go to Ur with Isaac to find him a suitable wife.

The servant and Isaac set off with a train of camels. The servant left Isaac behind on the journey and went on to the city of Nahor. At sundown the servant took the camels to the wells outside the city, where the women came out to fill their pitchers with water. Abraham's servant stood there and prayed that God would help him to find a wife for Isaac, as Abraham had instructed him. He prayed that God would indicate to him one of the young women at the well, and then he, the servant, would say to her, 'Please give me a drink, and drink for my camels also.' If she said yes, he would know that she was the woman God had chosen for Isaac.

Just then he saw a very beautiful young woman come to the well to fill her pitcher. (He did not know it, but she was a distant relative of Abraham.) Her name was Rebekah.

He said to her, 'May I drink a little water from your jug?' (In a hot dry country, it was a common courtesy to give water to others.)

She took down the pitcher from her shoulder and said, 'Of course. Drink, my lord.' When he had drunk his fill, she said, 'You will need water for your camels,' and she filled her pitcher several times at the well and poured the water into the animal trough so that the camels could drink.

The servant said, 'Is there a place here where I could stay?'

And Rebekah said, 'There is room in the house of my father Bethuel, and straw and food enough for the camels.' And the servant gave her gold bracelets and earrings in payment.

Rebekah ran home, and told her family what had happened, and her brother Laban went out to meet the servant. He took him in and welcomed him, and arranged for the camels to be stabled.

But Abraham's servant said, 'Before I eat, there is something I must tell you. I was sent here by Abraham, whom you will know of, since he came from here. God has made him very great and very wealthy in my own land, though he is now too old to come all this way himself. Abraham has a son, Isaac, who is of an age to marry, and Abraham wishes him to find a wife among his own people. He sent me here to find a wife for him, and I prayed to God to help me and to indicate a woman of his choice. God chose Rebekah.' And he explained to them how that had happened.

Laban answered and said, 'It seems this is what God has chosen,' and they sat up all night discussing the matter. The servant brought out the jewels and beautiful clothes that Abraham had sent for Isaac's future wife. Laban sent for Rebekah and asked for her agreement to marry Isaac, and she agreed.

All this while, Isaac had been waiting in a neighbouring city. He was still grieving for the loss of his mother, and took little interest in the servant's efforts to find him a wife. He was reflecting and grieving by himself one evening out in the fields when he looked up and saw a train of camels in the distance, and realised that they were his father's camels and that the servant was with them.

When Rebekah was told that the man in the field was Isaac, her future husband, she covered her face with her veil and got down off her camel and went towards him. And the servant went with her and explained to Isaac all that had happened.

From this first meeting Isaac felt very drawn to Rebekah, and had an immediate sense of being comforted for the loss of his mother. He took her home to meet Abraham, and then Rebekah became his wife. They loved each other deeply.

Genesis 25–28

Isaac and Rebekah
have twin sons

Jacob receives his brother's birthright

Jacob's ladder

JACOB AND ESAU

Jacob meets Rachel at the well

Jacob marries Leah and,
after seven years, Rachel

Jacob and Esau are reunited

Genesis 29-33

JACOB AND ESAU

Abraham died a very old man, and was given a loving burial by Ishmael and Isaac. Ishmael had had many children, just as God had promised, but Isaac and Rebekah as yet had none. After some years, however, Rebekah conceived, and she believed that she was expecting twins. It felt as if two children were struggling together inside her. When she asked God in prayer, God told her that, yes, she would have twin sons, and that one of them, the younger, would be much more powerful than the other, though they would each be the father of many children.

The twins were born, first Esau, a powerful, red-haired child whose whole body was covered in hair, then Jacob, who was born so soon after his brother that he was clutching his heel as he came out of the womb. As the two boys grew up, Esau loved to be out of doors, chasing and hunting, whereas Jacob was happier sitting quietly at home in his tent or helping with the animals. Esau was Isaac's favourite, and the old man liked to eat the wild game which he brought home from hunting. Jacob, however, was Rebekah's favourite.

One day Jacob made a stew of lentils which smelled wonderful. Esau came home starving after a day's hunting and he said to Jacob, 'Quick! Give me some of that stew. I am beside myself with hunger.'

Jacob, who had a greedy, cunning streak, replied, 'Only if you promise to give me your birthright.' The birthright was the special privileges that Esau enjoyed as the elder son. Esau was famished with hunger and probably thought, even when Jacob made him swear to give him the birthright, that he was joking, so he said, 'Yes, all right, you can have my birthright.' So Jacob gave his brother the bread and the stew that he craved, and Esau went on his way. But Jacob soon made him aware that he had meant what he said about taking Esau's birthright.

As his life went on, Isaac, their father, became a very rich and successful man. But eventually he grew old and blind, and knew that he was near to death. One day he sent for Esau and begged him to take his bow and arrows and go out hunting for wild game, so that he might taste his favourite dish once more before he died. Isaac said that as soon as he had eaten it he would give Esau his blessing, a solemn ritual in those days between father and son, rather like people making a will in our own day.

Rebekah overheard this conversation, and as soon as she had seen Esau safely off on his hunting trip she called Jacob, repeated what Isaac had said and told Jacob that he must do exactly as she told him.

'Go and fetch two kids from the flock and kill them. I will prepare them in just the way that your father likes. You will take the dish in to him, pretending to be Esau, and he is so blind and confused that he will give you his blessing instead of Esau.'

Jacob was slightly shocked at this suggestion, but he was even more afraid that if he followed Rebekah's plan he would be found out.

'I don't have to remind you, Mother, that Esau has a very hairy skin. If I embrace my father he will notice this and will guess what I am doing. If I am not careful, instead of blessing me he will curse me.' (A father's curse was a very terrible thing.)

Rebekah replied, 'If there are any curses, let them fall upon me. Do as I tell you!'

So Jacob fetched the kids and killed them,

and his mother prepared one of his father's favourite dishes. Then she dressed Jacob in his brother's clothes, and she put the goats' skins over Jacob's hands and his neck. She gave Jacob the dish of meat and the bread to take in to his father. Jacob carried it in to the old man and said, 'Father!'

Isaac said, 'Who is it?'

Jacob replied, 'Esau. I have done just as you told me. Come and eat the game that I have prepared for you.'

Isaac felt that something was wrong. 'How did you do this so quickly?' he asked.

'Because God helped me with my hunting.'

'Come here!' said Isaac, 'and let me hold you.' Jacob went near and Isaac touched him, and then he said, puzzled, 'The voice is the voice of Jacob, but the hands are Esau's hands.' The hairy hands, however, eventually persuaded Isaac that this must indeed be Esau.

So Isaac ate the meat and drank the wine. He asked Jacob to kiss him, and when he did so he could smell the familiar smell of the fields that he associated with Esau. So he gave him his solemn father's blessing, which was the right of the eldest son, wishing him power and wealth and many children, and calling down curses upon the head of any who ill-used him. Jacob left him and went away.

Almost immediately Esau came in from hunting, bearing the cooked meat his father had craved. He begged his father to eat and then to give him his blessing.

Isaac replied, 'Who are you?'

Esau said, 'I am your son, your firstborn, Esau.'

Isaac began to tremble in great distress and said, 'But who was it who came here and brought me meat? I ate the meat and then gave him my solemn blessing.'

Esau guessed what had happened and cried out in pain, 'Bless me, too, my father!'

Isaac said, 'I fear that your brother Jacob has deceived me and stolen the blessing that should have been for you, my firstborn son.'

'That's twice he has cheated me!' Esau cried. 'Have you no blessing for me?'

Isaac said that he had already made Jacob lord of everything he owned, and he did not know what to do. Esau wept in agony. Isaac said that Esau too should have wealth, but that he should be dominated by his brother unless he became powerful enough to overcome him. Esau was so angry that he swore he would kill Jacob.

Rebekah overheard Esau's vow and sent secretly for Jacob to warn him. Hoping that Esau's anger would soon die down, she told Esau to go and visit her brother Laban in Canaan, and then when she thought it was safe she would send him word to return.

JACOB'S DREAM

Appalled at what had happened, and frightened of his brother Esau, Jacob set off to visit his uncle Laban feeling utterly wretched. It was a long journey, and when it grew dark and he could no longer see to travel, he lay down on the desert floor to sleep, with a stone for a pillow. At once he began to dream, and in the dream he saw a ladder which stood upon the earth but which reached up to heaven. Angels flew up and down it. From high in the heavens he could hear the voice of God, saying, 'I am the God of Abraham and Isaac, of your father and grandfather, and I am your God too. This land I give to you and to your descendants, and they shall be a blessing to the whole earth. I will be with you, and protect you, and will see that you return to this land.'

Jacob woke up, overwhelmed by the power of his dream, and he said to himself, 'Surely God is present in this place, and I did not realise it! This very spot is the house of God and the gate of heaven.' He picked up the stone he had used for his head and put it on top of a pillar of stone, and he poured oil upon it as an offering to God. He called the place Bethel. In spite of Jacob's wrongdoing, in his time of desperation God had called him, and Jacob felt a great gratitude for God's promise to protect him. He swore a vow that if he returned one day to his father's house in peace, he would give a tenth of his wealth to God and to the poor.

JACOB MEETS RACHEL

So Jacob travelled on to Haran, where his uncle Laban lived. As he approached he saw a well with flocks of sheep surrounding it, and shepherds with them. He started talking to the shepherds, and soon discovered that they came from Haran and knew Laban well.

'And look!' they said. 'Here is his daughter Rachel bringing his sheep to be watered!' As soon as Jacob saw Rachel, his cousin, he was deeply attracted to her. He kissed her, wept with emotion and told her who he was, and then he pushed back the stone at the mouth of the well for her, so that she could water her sheep. Rachel ran home to tell her father that Jacob, Rebekah's son, had arrived. Laban ran out to greet him, and kissed him and took him home to be a guest in his house.

In the days that followed, Jacob helped with the work of the farm and fell more and more deeply in love with Rachel. When Laban offered to pay him for his work, he said that what he would like would be to earn the right to marry one of his daughters. Laban had two daughters – the elder, Leah, and the younger, Rachel. Laban wanted Jacob to marry Leah, since it was not the custom in that country for a younger sister to marry before an older sister, but Jacob only had eyes for Rachel.

'Stay and work for me for seven years,' said Laban, 'and you shall marry my daughter.'

Jacob was so passionately in love with Rachel that he would have done anything, and he served Laban gladly and well. The time passed quickly because he was so happy.

At the end of seven years he said to Laban, 'The time is fulfilled. Give me my wife.'

Laban put on a great feast and invited all his friends, and when it was dark and Jacob was in bed, he took Leah in to him and said, 'Here is your wife!' Jacob made love to Leah, thinking it

was Rachel, and when the morning came he was horrified to realise the trick Laban had played on him.

Laban insisted that Jacob must keep Leah as his wife, and then serve another seven years to take Rachel as his second wife. Since Jacob needed Laban's consent, there was nothing he could do but obey. Finally, after another seven years of hard work, Jacob married Rachel.

Of course, Jacob made it plain he did not love Leah as he loved Rachel, and, pitying Leah, God gave her six sons and one daughter. For a long while Rachel had no children, which was a great grief to her. Eventually, however, Rachel did have a child, a boy, Joseph.

All the while that Jacob had been with Laban he had been homesick for his own home and country, and finally he told Laban that he wanted to return home with his wives and children and a share of the cattle and sheep he had helped to rear. During Jacob's stay with him, Laban had become very prosperous, and this was largely due to Jacob's efforts. Laban begged Jacob to remain, and when he saw that he would not, tried to play a trick on him in dividing up the cattle they had reared together in such a way that Jacob would get only sick and deformed animals.

Jacob managed to outwit Laban over the animals, but he was fearful of what else Laban might do to get his own way. Even Rachel and Leah agreed that Laban had behaved badly and that their sympathies were with Jacob and not with their father. So finally the three of them set off secretly to his father Isaac's house, accompanied by many servants and camels and farm animals.

As he drew nearer to his old home, Jacob became fearful of Esau, and he sent a message to him by a servant telling him all that had happened and that he hoped to find grace in his brother's sight. Back came the message that Esau was riding out to meet him with four hundred men. Jacob was terrified. In desperation he prayed to God to help him.

Then he decided to prepare a present for his brother, and he chose many goats and sheep and camels, with their young. He told his servants to set off ahead of the rest of the party, and when they met Esau to tell him that the animals were a present for him from his brother.

Beside himself with fear, that night Jacob went away by himself to pray, and suddenly a man appeared who began to fight him. They wrestled furiously together for hours, and as the sun came up the man touched Jacob and wounded his thigh. Jacob begged the man (who was really an angel) to let him go.

'What is your name?' asked the angel.

'Jacob.'

'After this you will also be known as Israel.' (The people descended from Jacob would all carry this name.) Jacob called the place Peniel, which meant that this was the place where he had seen God face to face and survived. As he set off to meet Esau, the sun

came up. Jacob limped, because of the injury to his thigh.

He now went on to meet Esau with a lighter heart, but to be on the safe side he put Rachel and Joseph at the back of the train of camels, so that they might be protected if Esau attacked them. But Esau did no such thing. As Jacob and his servants got down from their camels and bowed low before him, he put his arms round Jacob and hugged him and wept. God had been good to Esau in the years Jacob had been away, and he no longer chose to remember the old injury he had done him. So Jacob and his family went to Succoth and built a house and made stables for the cattle, and then, deeply grateful to God, Jacob built an altar and sacrificed in the place where he had once been poor and frightened.

Genesis 37

Joseph becomes his father's favourite

Reuben pleads for Joseph

Joseph is thrown into the pit

Joseph is sold into slavery

Potiphar buys Joseph in Egypt

Joseph and His Brothers

Jacob had twelve sons altogether by his wives and maidservants, but his favourite was Joseph, the child of Rachel whom he loved. The other, older, sons always resented the fact that Joseph was the favourite. When Joseph was seventeen his father gave him the most beautiful coat, made in many different colours, which his brothers deeply envied. Unknown to Joseph and Jacob, the brothers' feelings of envy were turning to hatred, and they plotted against Joseph, though he remained unaware of how angry they were.

He often had dreams which he would describe when he woke up, not realising how much his brothers felt irritated by the habit. One day he insisted on telling his brothers about the most remarkable dream he had just had.

'We were all out in the fields binding the sheaves of corn at harvest,' he told them, 'when my sheaf suddenly stood upright and your sheaves all bowed down in front of it.'

Naturally his brothers did not like the sound of this. 'So you think you are going to reign over us, do you?' they said. 'Even though we are older than you, you think you can tell us what to do?' They disliked Joseph more than ever. The dream suggested to them that he was very proud of himself, and it felt like the last straw.

Very soon after this Joseph innocently reported another dream. 'It was extraordinary,' he said. 'This time the sun and the moon and eleven stars all bowed in front of me.'

Jacob, his father, thought he knew what was going on in Joseph's mind, and though he loved his son very much he was almost as resentful as the brothers

had been. 'I suppose you like the idea of me and your mother and brothers all bowing in front of you, do you? I'm surprised at you. You are letting your imagination run away with you, my son.'

It was usual at certain seasons of the year for the sheep to be taken to pastures where there was better food for them. All the sons except Joseph took Jacob's flocks and rode with them to Shechem, while Joseph remained at home with his father.

One day Jacob sent for Joseph and asked him to go to Shechem to see how his brothers and the animals were faring, and he agreed and set off. He could not find his brothers at Shechem, however. By chance he met a man on the road and asked if he had seen them, and the man said that he had met them and talked to them, and they had moved the flock on to another place where the grazing was better.

So Joseph set off after them. His brothers had already been discussing him scornfully in his absence, saying to one another how much they loathed him, and how they wished he would die so that they could be rid of him. When they saw him in the distance, one of them said nastily, 'Look, here comes the dreamer!'

Another one said, perhaps partly as a joke, 'Let's kill him, throw him into a pit, and say some wild animal attacked him. That should take care of his dreams!' The others at once seized on the idea.

Reuben, the oldest brother and the most compassionate, was horrified at their cruelty and tried to think of a way to save Joseph.

'I have a better idea,' he said. 'Let us not have the blood of our brother on our hands. Let us cast him into a pit where he cannot climb out, and let the wild animals do what they will with him.'

Secretly, Reuben thought that he would come back later and help Joseph out of the pit, and send him home to Jacob.

The brothers agreed to do what Reuben suggested, and when Joseph reached them, before he could so much as greet them, they had grabbed hold of him, stripped him of his coat of many colours and thrown him into a deep hole in the ground from which he had no hope of climbing out. He was terrified and very surprised. It had never occurred to him that his brothers hated him so much. Reuben had left them before Joseph arrived, to see to the flock.

The other brothers sat down to eat their midday meal and to consider what to do next. Soon a group of merchants from Gilead came along, carrying spices, balm and myrrh on their camels, which they hoped to sell in Egypt. Judah, one of the brothers, said, 'Why don't we sell Joseph to them as a slave? That way, his blood will not be on our hands. He is our brother, after all, and, much though we dislike him, it would be wrong for us to kill him.'

The others all agreed with him. So the brothers pulled Joseph up out of the pit and sold him to the merchants for twenty pieces of silver, though he pleaded with them to be merciful to him.

After a while Reuben returned and went to look in the pit, perhaps to feed Joseph or to help him out, but there was no sign of him. Thinking an animal had taken him, he began to grieve, and tore his clothes in his anguish. He went back to his brothers and cried out, 'Joseph has gone! What shall we do?' They told him what they had done.

One of the brothers suggested that if they took Joseph's coat of many colours and dipped it in animal's blood, it would look as if Joseph had been taken by a wild creature. So they dipped Joseph's coat in blood and carried it back to Jacob, saying artfully, 'We are very worried. We have not seen Joseph, but we found this coat stained in blood which looks very like the one which you gave to him.'

At once Jacob recognised it as the coat he had given to Joseph, and he burst out in an agony of crying and tore his clothes and dressed himself in sackcloth, and went on grieving for many days. 'Joseph, my beloved son, has been torn to pieces!' he mourned.

The brothers, who saw the effect that their wicked actions had had, tried to comfort him, and Jacob's daughters also tried, but it was no use. Jacob was heartbroken. 'I shall go down to the grave mourning for Joseph,' he said, weeping. 'Nothing can comfort me.'

Meanwhile the merchants had travelled on to Egypt, and had sold Joseph as a slave there to a man called Potiphar, who served in Pharaoh's household and was a captain of the guard. Potiphar at once took a liking to Joseph – he could see that he was intelligent and honourable and came of a good family – and he decided to make him, young as he was, the overseer of his household.

Genesis 39-44

Potiphar's wife accuses Joseph

Joseph is sent to prison

Joseph interprets the Pharaoh's dreams

Joseph finds the cup in Benjamin's sack

JOSEPH IN EGYPT

Joseph prospered in Potiphar's household and was trusted by his master.

Unfortunately, however, Potiphar's wife was attracted to him, and invited him to come into her bed and make love to her, which was very wrong of her. Joseph refused her, but one day, when he was alone in the house with her, she tried to embrace him. He slipped away, leaving his cloak in her hand, and left the house.

When Potiphar came home she pretended that exactly the opposite had happened – that Joseph had tried to force her to make love with him. She showed her husband the cloak. Potiphar was very angry that Joseph had, as he thought, betrayed his trust, and had him thrown into prison.

Two important officials happened to be in prison at the same time, one of them Pharaoh's butler, the man who was in charge of his domestic servants, and the other Pharaoh's baker. Both of them had remarkable dreams. They confided them to Joseph, who interpreted them. He said that the butler's dream, which was about pouring wine into the Pharaoh's cup, meant that in three days he should be restored to favour with the Pharaoh. Joseph begged him, when that day came, to ask Pharaoh to release him from prison. The baker's dream, however, which was about birds stealing food he had prepared, meant that in three days the baker would die.

All happened as Joseph said, but the butler conveniently forgot about Joseph when he got his old job back. Two years later, Pharaoh himself had a very remarkable dream. He stood by the Nile, and from it there came seven fine, strong, well-fed cattle, which started to feed in a mead-ow. After them came seven thin, sickly cattle. Then he dreamed again, first of seven plump ears of corn all growing thickly on one stalk, and then of seven thin, wasted-looking ears of corn which looked as if the east wind had blasted them.

The Pharaoh felt uneasy. He sent for all the wise men of Egypt, hoping that one of them could give him a convincing interpretation, but nobody seemed able to make sense of the dreams. Suddenly the butler remembered the young man who had so accurately interpreted dreams in the prison, and he told his master the story. Pharaoh sent at once for Joseph.

Pharaoh described his two dreams and Joseph listened carefully. Finally he said, 'They are really one dream in which God is warning you. They describe seven years of plenty followed by seven years of famine. The famine will be a terrible one. What you must do is select an overseer to make sure that you store plenty of grain during the good years, so that during the famine Egypt will have enough to eat.'

Pharaoh knew at once that Joseph spoke the truth. Like Potiphar before him, he was impressed with Joseph's wisdom, and he decided to appoint him as his overseer. He took off his ring and put it on Joseph's hand as a symbol of power, and he ordered fine clothes for him and a gold chain of office. The man who had been in prison only the day before was suddenly raised to great power and could have anything he wished.

Joseph took his new job very seriously, and in every city he had a huge barn built in which food could be stored. Since the harvests were very plentiful it was not difficult.

After seven years the famine came at last, not only in Egypt but in all the countries round about.

Meanwhile Jacob and his family in Canaan were very

short of food. Hearing of Egypt's plenty, Jacob sent all his sons except the youngest, Benjamin, to Egypt to try to buy corn. He loved Benjamin dearly, and after losing Joseph would not let him out of his sight.

The brothers went to Egypt and were shown into Joseph's presence. He recognised them at once, though they did not recognise him. He pretended that he could not speak their language and talked to them through an interpreter. He spoke harshly to them, saying he believed them to be spies, and he had them interrogated. This gave him the chance to find out all about his family, and to discover that Jacob was still alive. He overheard them saying to one another that this experience was a punishment to them for treating Joseph so badly. They mentioned the youngest brother at home, Benjamin, his father's favourite. Joseph said he would let them go, but would keep just one of them, Simeon, as a hostage. He would not release him unless they returned with Benjamin. Joseph gave them the corn they needed, but secretly hid the money that they paid him in their sacks of corn. They were very puzzled when they found it later, and thought perhaps it was a trick to accuse them of stealing.

The brothers returned to Jacob and poured out the strange story. Jacob was very upset. 'First I lose my beloved Joseph, now I lose Simeon, and soon I may lose Benjamin.' And he wept.

At first he refused to let Benjamin go away, but soon they were again short of food and he knew that his sons would have to go back to Egypt. Judah promised to take care of Benjamin and to do everything possible to make sure he came to no harm. Jacob suggested that they took presents for the overseer of Egypt – spices, balm, myrrh, nuts and honey.

When Joseph learned that they had arrived he gave orders for a feast to be prepared in his house at noon. The brothers were very afraid when they were taken there, fearing that they were about to be killed. But Joseph's steward welcomed them and brought Simeon out to greet them. Nervously, they laid out their presents.

When Joseph came in they bowed low before him and he asked after their father. At the same time his eyes fell upon Benjamin and he felt a great love for him well up, and had to leave the room to weep, he was so moved. A feast was laid before them by Joseph's servants, with special dishes.

While they ate, Joseph commanded that each brother should be given a sack of corn with his money tucked inside it as before, but that in Benjamin's sack should be hidden Joseph's own special drinking cup of silver. The brothers set happily off home, but they were scarcely out of the city before Joseph's servant caught up with them and, on Joseph's instructions, accused them of stealing a cup after being generously entertained in Joseph's house. Naturally they denied it. The servant searched through all their baggage, and when he came to Benjamin's sack, last of all, there was the cup.

The brothers were terrified. They were taken back to Joseph's house, where they fell on the ground before Joseph. Joseph pretended to be very stern with them, and said that they could go home but that because of his theft Benjamin must remain. In desperation the brothers poured out the whole family history – Jacob's grief at the loss of Joseph, his love for Benjamin and fear of losing him, their own promises to take care of him.

Finally, Joseph could bear it no longer. He sent away his servants, but began to weep in so loud a voice that he could be heard all over the house.

'I am your brother Joseph,' he said at last.

The brothers did not know what to say, they were so ashamed. But Joseph told them that it was not they, but God, who had sent him to Egypt to foresee the great famine. He told them to go home and tell Jacob that he was still alive and that he had achieved great things in Egypt. Then they were to bring Jacob and his household back to Egypt while the famine lasted. His brothers begged his pardon over and over again, he asked them many questions about life at home, and they stayed up late talking and embracing one another.

Exodus 1-7

The Pharaoh's daughter finds
baby Moses

Moses kills the Egyptian

The Burning Bush

Moses and Aaron go to see
the Pharaoh

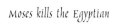

The plagues of Egypt

Moses leads the Israelites
through the Red Sea

Exodus 7-15

THE STORY OF THE EXODUS

Many years passed, and the Israelites who had remained in Egypt were no longer liked and protected by the new Pharaoh. The Egyptian people were jealous of their prosperity, and they started forcing the Israelites to do hard labour for them, building the huge cities they were constructing. Worst of all, they issued an ultimatum that their boy babies should be killed at birth.

One Israelite woman secretly gave birth to a boy baby. She hid him in her house for three months, fearful that his crying would give him away. Then she made a cradle of bulrushes and covered it with slime and pitch, so that it would float like a little boat. She put the baby inside it, and placed it at the river's edge. She told her little girl, Miriam, to play by the water in order to see what happened and then report back to her.

Soon the Pharaoh's daughter came down to bathe in the river. She noticed the floating cradle and wondered what it was. When she saw the little baby, she knew at once that it was an Israelite baby in danger of its life. The child began to cry bitterly, and the princess was moved. Her maid said, 'Shall I fetch one of the Israelite woman to be his wetnurse?' (A wetnurse was a woman who suckled a baby for its mother.) The princess agreed, and the maid asked Miriam if she knew a suitable woman. Miriam ran home and fetched her mother. So the baby's mother cared for him herself.

As soon as he was old enough, however, the baby had to go back to the palace, where the princess brought him up as her own son. She called him Moses, which meant 'drawn from the water'.

So Moses grew up in the Pharaoh's palace, and lived the life of an Egyptian prince. Yet he had a feeling, a memory perhaps, that this was not the whole truth about himself.

It troubled him that the Egyptians treated the Israelites so cruelly. One day he came across an Egyptian beating an Israelite worker, and in a fit of rage he struck down the Egyptian and killed him. He thought that no one had seen him, but news of it got to the Pharaoh's ears, and he threatened to kill Moses. Moses escaped to Midian, where he worked for a man called Jethro and eventually married his daughter, Zipporah.

Moses was minding Jethro's sheep in the desert near Mount Sinai one day when he saw an amazing thing. He saw a bush with fire pouring out of it, yet the bush remained green and undamaged. He stopped and stared, and then, from the heart of the bush, he heard a voice calling him: 'Moses! Moses!'

Moses said, 'I am here.'

'Come no closer,' said the voice. 'Take your shoes off. You are on holy ground. I am the God of your fathers, of Abraham, Isaac and Jacob.'

Moses suddenly felt very afraid and covered his face, not daring to look. God told him then that he was grieved at the sufferings of Israel and had decided that they must leave Egypt and return to Canaan, the land of milk and honey, as it was known. God said that he was sending Moses to persuade the Israelites that it was time to go, and to negotiate with Pharaoh.

Now Moses was afraid for a different reason. Who was he to challenge a great king like Pharaoh? It would be suicide. Why should the Israelites believe him, anyway?

'What shall I say to them?' Moses asked helplessly.

'Say that the God of their people

sent you,' said God.

'Who is that?' said Moses, who had not been brought up as an Israelite.

'I AM THAT I AM,' said God. 'Tell the people that I AM sent you.'

'Pharaoh won't let the people go,' said Moses.

'Yes, he will,' said God, 'but not immediately. I shall force him to do so.'

'I don't think I can persuade the people,' said Moses. 'And I dare not go and argue with Pharaoh. I have a stammer, and public speaking terrifies me.'

Moses kept on making excuses, which made God angry. In the end God said that Moses' brother Aaron, who was a wonderful speaker, could help him out.

Together Moses and Aaron went and told the Israelites about the plan for them to leave Egypt and travel to Canaan. Instead of scoffing, as Moses had feared, the people believed all that Moses and Aaron said, and were delighted at God's love for them.

Next, greatly fearing, Moses and Aaron went to see the Pharaoh, and told him that God had directed that his people must be allowed to leave Egypt. Pharaoh replied that the God of Israel meant nothing to him and he was not prepared to let the Israelites go. Moses said that he would tell the people to stop making bricks and to pray and sacrifice to God instead. This made Pharaoh very angry, and he commanded the overseers to work the people much harder and force them to hunt for stubble to make their bricks instead of having straw provided, yet to produce as many bricks as before. If they did not produce as many bricks as before they would be beaten.

So God sent a series of plagues upon the Egyptians, each worse than the last. He turned all the water in Egypt into blood, so that the Egyptians had nothing to drink, and sent a plague of frogs that overran people's houses. He sent lice, and flies, and a terrible disease that killed all the livestock, and painful boils.

After each plague Moses went to see Pharaoh. Sometimes he was angry and determined not to let the people go. Sometimes he pretended he was sorry and that he would let them go, but as soon as the plague was removed he changed his mind again. The slave workers were too useful to lose. Even when his advisers told Pharaoh to release the Israelites before Egypt was destroyed, he would not. He forbade Moses to come again into his presence.

There was one more devastating plague destined to fall upon Egypt. This was the killing of the firstborn – every firstborn Egyptian child, including that of the Pharaoh, and the firstborn of every animal.

The Israelites, under Moses' instruction, were preparing to depart. Each family killed a lamb and roasted it for a last meal, spreading its blood on the lintel of their house. Each of them got dressed in warm clothes and strong shoes and carried a staff, all ready to go.

None of them, Moses said, must leave their house until morning. In the night, the angel of God would pass through Egypt killing the firstborn, but sparing those houses with blood on the lintel.

There was a terrible outcry in Egypt that night as they discovered the dead firstborn. While the Egyptians were wailing and mourning, the Israelites quietly left Egypt with their flocks and herds. They took unleavened bread with them. This night was known as the night of the Passover (because the angel of death passed them over), and it is observed by Jews to this day.

The Israelites set off, Moses carrying the bones of Joseph, and God led them through the desert to the Red Sea.

Soon Pharaoh realised they had gone and chased after them in great anger with six hundred chariots. The Israelites realised with horror that they were trapped by the Red Sea, and they turned angrily upon Moses. Moses, however, lifted up his staff over the sea. A great wind sprang up and parted the waters, and the Israelites walked safely through the middle, a great wall of water on each side. The chariots and horsemen of Pharaoh raced after them, but the waters came together after the Israelites had passed, and the army of the Egyptians was drowned.

Exodus 16–20

God feeds the Israelites in
the desert

Moses receives the Ten Commandments

Arriving at the Promised
Land with the Ark

Exodus 32

The Golden Calf is idolised

Numbers 13

Balaam's ass

Numbers 22-24

Moses in the Desert

At first the Israelites were overjoyed at having escaped from Pharaoh's armies, and Moses and Miriam led them in songs of joy at their freedom. But after a few days, when they could find no water and their supplies of food began to run out, they began to find life in the desert very hard. They were missing their homes in Egypt. They felt angry with Moses and Aaron for persuading them to leave, and they accused them of having brought them and their children into the desert to die.

At last they came across twelve wells, where they could quench their thirst and give water to their animals, but food had become very scarce. God told Moses, however, that to show his care for the people, he would give them bread from heaven every morning. It would fall like rain upon them. Each day they should go out and gather just enough for their needs, but no more. On the sixth day they should gather twice as much as usual, so that they would have enough for the sabbath, the day that they rested as God had commanded. Every evening, God said, he would provide meat to go with their bread.

The people did not really believe Moses when he told them this, but the next morning, as the dew disappeared, small white pieces of bread lay on the ground. Tentatively they tasted it. It was like no bread they had ever eaten before; it was delicious, like honey, and they called it 'manna'. In the evening plump little birds called quails came to the camp of the Israelites, and they caught them and ate them. Whatever the hardships of life in the desert, it did not look as if God was going to let them starve.

Thirst was still a problem, however, once they had left the oasis, and their skins and gourds of water began to be used up. In spite of the manna and the quails, the Israelites became frightened, and because they were frightened they became angry. One day they were so angry about the lack of water that Moses thought they were about to stone him, and he begged God for help. God told him to stand before a great rock on Mount Sinai and to take his staff and strike it. Moses did so, and water gushed out, so that they could all fill their drinking vessels and the troughs for the animals.

Gradually the Israelites became used to their difficult wandering life as they travelled towards Canaan.

God told Moses, as he had told his great forebears Abraham, Isaac and Jacob, that he had chosen this people to have a special relationship with him. They were what he called his 'treasure'. He said that in three days' time he would descend upon Mount Sinai in a thick cloud; they would hear his voice but would not, with the exception of Moses, be able to see him (and Moses would only see a little – it was too overwhelming for a human being to see God). Before this event, however, the Israelites must wash themselves, put on clean clothes and pray, in order to prepare themselves. None of them must touch the mountain, except Moses.

On the third morning there was a great storm, with terrifying lightning and thunder, and what sounded like a trumpet. It was so loud that everyone began to tremble. Moses marched the people towards the foot of Mount Sinai for their meeting with God. The mountain was covered in smoke and flames, and the ground shook as if in an earthquake. God was upon the top of the mountain, in the smoke and flames.

As they heard the thunder and saw the lightning on the mountain, and felt the ground shake and heard the great trumpet, the people of Israel became very frightened and began to move away from the mountain. They said to Moses, 'Do not let God speak to us – we don't like it. You can speak to him on our behalf, and tell us what he says.'

Moses said to them, 'There is no need to be afraid.' He climbed the mountain alone and moved into the thick darkness where God was waiting for him.

God told Moses that his people, his treasure, whom he had delivered from Egypt, must choose to live good lives, loving and respecting God, and loving and respecting each other. There were ten basic rules, which later they called the Ten Commandments. The Israelites must first make a beautiful wooden container, decorated with gold and carvings of cherubim, to be called the Ark of the Covenant, which would hold the two stones on which the Commandments would be inscribed. It would be their holiest possession. The Ten Commandments of God would be as follows:

1 They must worship no other God but the God of Israel.
2 They must not make stone or metal gods or goddesses for themselves, in the shape of humans or animals, and then start to worship them.
3 They must not use God's holy name loosely, or carelessly, or without respect, as if it meant nothing.
4 They should continue to keep the seventh day of the week as the sabbath, a day of rest and rejoicing, in memory of God's own day of rest when he created the world.
5 They should love and respect the father and mother who brought them into the world and cared for them as children.
6 They should not commit murder.

7 They should not steal the husband or wife of another.
8 They should not steal other people's possessions.
9 They should not accuse their neighbours falsely and get them into trouble.
10 They should not let jealousy or envy of their neighbours enter their hearts.

Moses was gone for many hours. When he did not reappear, the people said to Aaron, 'We do not think we shall ever see him again. Goodness only knows what has become of him! That whole experience was a bit too much for us. What we need to do now to comfort ourselves is to make our own gods and carry them with us. That's a much better way.'

Aaron, who was no happier than they were, said, 'Give me all the gold that you have.' The women took off their golden earrings and gave them to Aaron, and he heated the gold in the fire until it melted and moulded it into a calf. He presented the calf to them and said, 'Here is the god that brought you out of Egypt.' He built an altar and declared the next day a feast day.

The next day the people got up and offered sacrifices to the golden calf, and then began to eat and drink and enjoy themselves, while Moses remained up on the mountain, alone with God.

God spoke to Moses urgently. 'Go down at once, Moses. The people you brought out of Egypt have turned from worshipping me to worshipping an idol, and I am very angry with them. I am so angry that I am afraid I shall wish to destroy them, and they will never become the great nation I wanted them to be.'

Finding this hard to believe, Moses made his way down the mountain, carrying the two tablets of stone on which the Ten Commandments were engraved. As he got nearer to the camp he heard music and singing, and he saw the golden calf set up on high, where all the people could see it. As he got closer still, he could see the people dancing naked before the statue.

Worn out with his journey, and deeply disappointed, Moses suddenly became very angry. He threw the tablets of stone down on the ground so hard that they broke in pieces. Then he marched furiously into the camp. He took the golden calf and threw it into the fire, and when it was molten he stamped it into powder and forced some of the dancers to drink the powder in water.

He turned upon Aaron and said, 'How could you let the people sin like this? After all we have gone through, how could you?'

Aaron tried to explain how the people had thought that Moses was not coming back, and how they had forced him, Aaron, to make gods for them, but Moses would have none of it. He had the ringleaders killed, and went again to Sinai to beg God's forgiveness.

'If you cannot forgive them,' he prayed, 'then do not forgive me, either, but blot me out of the book of life.'

'I shall not forget what they did,' said God, 'but now, go and lead your people to the place I told you of. My angel shall go before you to help you.'

THE JOURNEY TO CANAAN

So the Israelites set off on the long journey once again. It took them many years, and many adventures, to reach Canaan. When they were in sight of it at last, Moses sent men to spy out the land, to see who lived there, what it was like and how they could settle there.

They had arrived during the grape harvest, and the men came back with clusters of grapes, figs and pomegranates. This confirmed the promise that Canaan would be a land of milk and honey and other good things.

Moses was by now very old and feeble, and God told him that he would not live to take the Israelites into the Promised Land. Joshua would lead the people in his place, crossing the River Jordan that lay between them and Canaan. The people must be brave and strong, because the inhabitants of Canaan would resist them, but in the end they would inhabit the land.

Moses sent for Joshua and told him that he must be strong and of good courage, because he was the chosen leader to take the Israelites into the land of Canaan.

Then God told Moses to go up into the mountains, so that, although he would never enter Canaan, he would at least be able to see the Promised Land. There on Mount Nebo, he told him, he would die and be gathered to his ancestors.

Very slowly Moses climbed the mountain. He could now see a vast expanse of land all the way to the sea, and to the south the valley of Jericho with its palm trees. It was all beautiful.

'Here it is, Moses,' said God, 'the land which I promised you.'

Moses died there on the mountain, having seen the Promised Land. There never was another prophet as great as Moses, who saw and spoke to God face to face.

THE STORY OF BALAAM AND HIS ASS

The people of Israel had many enemies when they first arrived in Canaan. Balak, the king of the Moabites, was angry when he saw hundreds of people arriving in his country from Egypt, and he sent a message to the prophet Balaam. He had great faith in Balaam's powers, and he wanted him to curse the newcomers and drive them away. He promised him a reward if he used his power to bring this about. The young princes of Moab, who were Balak's messengers, explained all this to Balaam, and he said to them, 'Stay the night, so that I may pray and think about what you say.'

In the night God spoke to Balaam and said, 'Who are these people?' Balaam explained about the princes and why they had come, and how they wanted him to go with them, curse the people of the Israelites and drive them out of the country.

'You must not go with these men,' said God, 'nor must you curse these people who have arrived here. They are a blessed people whom I have chosen.'

Next morning, Balaam said to the princes, 'I cannot come with you. My God will not allow it.'

The princes went back to Balak and told him what Balaam had said, but he refused to accept it and sent other older and grander princes to go back and reason with him.

'You must come at all costs. I will shower you with honours and wealth, but you must help me drive these interlopers away. I, your king, command it!'

Balaam did not know what to do. He replied to the princes, 'Even if Balak offered me his own house full of priceless silver and gold I could not go, because God has forbidden it.' He was beginning to waver, however, and told the princes to wait until morning in case God had more to say to him. Perhaps he hoped God would relent in the night. God, however, once again sternly forbade him to go with them.

When the morning came, Balaam weakened. He got up, saddled his ass and went with the princes of Moab. He was riding along, with two servants beside him, when all of a sudden his ass reared up and bolted into a field. Unknown to Balaam, the ass had seen an angel standing in front of him with a drawn sword.

Balaam was very cross and began to beat the ass. Then he rode it along a narrow road with walls on both sides. Once again the ass saw the angel right in front of him and bolted into the wall, crushing Balaam's foot against it, and once again an angry Balaam struck the ass. Finally, the angel stood right in front of the ass in such a narrow space that there was no escape, and this time the ass fell down on the ground in terror. This time Balaam struck her with his staff.

To his utter astonishment he then heard the ass speak. She said, 'Why have you beaten me three times when I have done nothing wrong?'

Balaam replied, 'Because you have been playing games with me, and you have hurt me. I am so angry with you I could kill you.'

The ass said, 'Am I not your faithful ass upon which you have ridden all these years, and have I ever behaved badly?' Balaam had to admit that she never had.

At that moment Balaam himself suddenly saw the angel of God with the sword in his hand, and he threw himself upon the ground and bowed his head into the dust.

The angel said, 'So why did you strike this poor beast when I tried to stop you doing wrong? Perhaps if she had not turned aside I should have struck you dead by now.'

Balaam said, 'I know that I have done wrong, though I did not know that it was you who stood in front of me. Should I go back home again?'

'No,' said the angel. 'Go with the princes now, but speak no word except what I shall tell you.'

When Balak heard that Balaam was coming, he rode out to meet him, chiding him for not coming sooner and for not doing as he asked him in cursing the Israelites.

Balaam told Balak to set up seven altars and prepare oxen and rams for sacrifice, and then God would tell them both what must be done about the newcomers.

God did speak to Balaam, but it was to tell him once again that he must not curse those whom God loved and wished to bless. Balak refused to listen when Balaam told him.

Finally, Balak and Balaam together arrived at the place where the Israelites were camped in hundreds in their tents. It had the opposite effect from what Balak intended. Balaam was very moved at the sight. He caught a glimpse of the vision that God had for Israel – a beautiful country inhabited by peace-loving people who were strong and just, and who loved God and cared for one another.

Balak became very angry and told the holy man to get out of his sight, and that none of the riches and honours that he had promised him would now be his. So Balaam, knowing that he had only done what God had commanded him, went back to his home, without gold or silver or the approval of his king, but feeling he had behaved honourably.

Joshua 2-6

Rahab hides Joshua's spies

The battle of Jericho

Jael kills Sisera

Gideon tests his soldiers

Abimelech and the millstone

Jephthah sees his daughter

Judges 4

Judges 6-7

Judges 9

Judges 11

THE PROMISED LAND

God said to Joshua, 'Moses, my servant, is dead. It is for you now to lead the people, to cross into Jordan with them, as I promised. Wherever your foot treads, from the desert and Lebanon as far as the River Euphrates and as far as the great sea westwards, is yours. I will be with you as I was with Moses. I will not fail you or forsake you, and no man shall be able to oppose you. But you will need to be brave and strong, and to meditate on the law that Moses gave you, so that the people do not go astray. Don't be afraid. I will be with you wherever you go, and whatever you do.'

Joshua at once instructed all the heads of the tribes of Israel: 'Go among your people and tell them to prepare food for a journey. Within three days we shall pass over Jordan and enter the land that God promised us.' He told the warriors of Israel that they must go first into the Promised Land to protect the people who followed them. Their wives and children and animals should remain behind and wait for them, and not cross over into Jordan yet. The army pledged themselves to obey him as they had obeyed Moses.

Then Joshua sent two men over into Jericho to act as spies. To avoid suspicion of their motive they went to lodge at the house of a prostitute, Rahab. The men were seen entering Rahab's house, and the king of Jericho sent soldiers there to search for them and arrest them, because he guessed they were spies. Before she let the soldiers in, Rahab whispered to the spies to go up and hide in the flax piled on her roof to dry.

'They were here,' she said to the soldiers, 'but I did not realise they were anyone special. They left before it was dark, presumably to get out of the city before the gates were shut. I don't know which way they went, but they have not been gone long. I think if you hurried you could catch up with them.'

The soldiers left quickly, going towards Jordan where they knew the Israelites were camped.

All this time the Israelite men were hiding among the flax on Rahab's roof.

Rahab returned to the men and said, 'They are gone. I know who you are, that your God has said that your people are to inherit this land; the people here are terrified of you. We heard how your God dried up the Red Sea to let you go free from Egypt. The people here know that they do not stand a chance against you, and believe they are all going to be killed. Because I was kind to you and saved your lives, will you promise to spare me and my family?' The men promised that they would see that she and her family were spared.

Rahab's house was built into the wall of the town, so that it was possible for her to let the men down by rope to a place outside the walls.

'Go and hide in the mountains for a few days until they have stopped looking for you,' she advised. The men told her to twine a scarlet thread in the window of her house so that the Israelites could identify it later, and to bring all her family into her house to be with her in safety. None of them must go out until the siege and the fighting were over.

The men climbed out of her window, and Rahab bound scarlet thread in the window of her house as they had told her. Eventually, by a roundabout route, the spies got back to Joshua and told him what had happened, and how terrified the inhabitants of

Jericho already were.

Joshua gave his orders to the people. When they saw the Ark of the Covenant, the carved box that held the sacred writings and vessels, carried in front of them, they should follow after it. Meanwhile, they should pray and prepare themselves for the wonders that God was about to show them.

The next day Joshua gave his instructions to the priests to take up the Ark of the Covenant and set off before the people. When they got to the brink of the River Jordan, he told them, they should wait there until the people were assembled behind them. The priests set off, and then Joshua spoke to the people, saying, 'The living God is among you and will take you safely into the Promised Land. You will see, if you doubted it, that our God is Lord over all the earth, for as the feet of the priests bearing the Ark of the Covenant touch the water, there will be a miracle.'

So the Israelites marched towards Jordan, the army going before them and the priests bearing the Ark of the Covenant going in front of them. As the feet of the priests carrying the Ark touched the waters of the Jordan, suddenly the waters parted, just as they had done many years before at the Red Sea, and first the priests, and then all the rest of the people of the Israelites, passed through the middle of the Jordan with dry feet.

They came up out of the river, and they camped at Gilgal. There they kept the feast of the Passover. For the first time since they had left Egypt God did not send them manna to eat. Instead, they used the corn of the country to make flour and bread.

Joshua walked by himself near to Jericho, and suddenly saw a man with a drawn sword in his hand standing in front of him. Joshua said to him, 'Are you my friend? Or my enemy?' The man said he was the captain of the hosts of the Lord, meaning that he was an angel. Joshua fell to the ground in awe of him and worshipped God, and asked him what he must do.

'Take off your shoes,' the angel said, just as an angel had once said to Jacob. 'The place where you stand is holy ground.'

The king of Jericho, like the king of Moab, had been very frightened when he heard how the Israelites had crossed the Jordan on dry land. He ordered that all the gates of the city of Jericho should be bolted and barred, so that no one could go in or out.

God, however, told Joshua that he intended him to take the city. He told him to encircle it with the Israelites, and to parade his army round the city of Jericho once a day for seven days. The men of war would be preceded by priests carrying the Ark of the Covenant, accompanied by seven priests blowing on rams' horns. On the seventh day they should make a very long blast on the rams' horns, and all the Israelites were to give a loud shout when they heard it, and then, all at once, the walls of the city would fall down flat.

The people did exactly as Joshua told them, and on the seventh day they encircled the city in total quietness, not even speaking a word. When they heard the long blast on the rams' horns they shouted with all their might, and as they did so the walls of the city of Jericho fell down flat. The Israelites entered the city and killed the inhabitants. They found all the silver, gold and precious objects, took them out of the city, and then set fire to Jericho and burned it to the ground. First, however, Joshua kept the promise to Rahab, the prostitute, and her family. They were allowed to escape and to make new lives in another town.

JAEL AND SISERA

The Israelites had many adventures in their new country. At one point, when they had not obeyed God's commandments, God allowed them to be enslaved by a king called Jabin, who reigned in a place called Hazor, and he oppressed them cruelly.

There was a holy woman called Deborah who lived quietly out in the desert. She was so wise that the Israelites used to come and consult her.

She sent for a warrior called Barak and said that God had shown her what they must do. Barak must assemble ten thousand Israelite soldiers and march on the River Sison, where he would meet and vanquish King Jabin's general Sisera.

This would only be part of the story, however. Sisera, Deborah prophesied, would be destroyed by the hand of a woman. Barak was uncertain what to do, but said that if Deborah would accompany him he would do as she said. He assembled his army, and when Sisera heard about it he assembled his own great army, which included nine hundred iron chariots.

'Now!' said Deborah. 'Now is the time for the battle!'

Barak and his army descended on Sisera's troops, and in a very short time they won a victory. In the heat of the battle, however, Sisera disappeared. He had slipped down from his chariot and fled away on foot.

Sisera went to the tent of a woman called Jael, whose husband was an ally of King Jabin. Jael, however, had no liking for the king and sympathised with the Israelites. Sisera was exhausted after the battle and wanted only to rest. Jael took Sisera in and made him comfortable, covering him with a cloak and begging him to sleep at his ease. She gave him food to eat and milk to drink.

'I beg you,' Sisera said to her, 'that when I am asleep, if any man comes to the door of the tent and asks you whether there is anyone within, that you say no.' Then he fell into a deep sleep.

Jael took a tent peg and a mallet, and going quietly to Sisera, struck the tent peg through his head with an almighty blow that fastened it into the ground, so that Sisera died instantly.

Jael went out and met Barak and said, 'Come. I will show you the man you seek.' Barak saw Sisera dead upon the ground, and knew that the Israelites were now free of the bondage of Jabin.

GIDEON

Another time the Israelites fell foul of a people called the Midianites, and sometimes they were so ill-treated by them that they fled away to hide in caves in the mountains. One day, however, an angel appeared to a man called Gideon as he worked on his father's land, and said to him, 'The Lord is with you, you mighty man of valour.'

Gideon said to the angel that he could not understand how it was that if God was with the Israelites so many dreadful things had befallen them. How was it that God had delivered them from Egypt only for them to fall into the power of the Midianites?

God then spoke. 'I have chosen you, strong man as you are, to save Israel from the Midianites.'

Gideon threw up his hands in despair. 'I come from a poor family, and I am the least important member of my family. How can I save anything?'

'Because I will help you,' said God. 'The men of Midian will be struck down at one blow.'

'It is so hard to believe,' said Gideon. 'I would like a sign that I am not dreaming this.'

He then went to prepare food as an offering to God, as was the custom – a kid, unleavened bread and broth. He put the meat and the bread on a rock, and poured the broth. Then the angel touched the meat and the bread with his staff, and immediately fire burst out of the rock and burned up all the food. It was an extraordinary sight.

Gideon was frightened at what he had seen – he thought he might die because he had seen an angel face to face, but God assured him that he was quite safe. Then God ordered him to destroy an altar to Baal and to the goddess Ashtaroth that his father had built on his land, and then to build an altar to God on which he must sacrifice a bullock. Gideon did this at night-time for fear of what his father and others might do.

In the morning, everyone saw that the altar of Baal had been torn down, and rumour leaked out that it was Gideon who had done it. An angry group of townspeople went to Gideon's father and told him to hand Gideon over to them so that they could kill him for committing such a crime. Unexpectedly, his father refused, saying that if Baal was a real god, he should be able to exact his own revenge and punish those who had offended him.

Suddenly Gideon felt himself filled with the spirit of God. He sounded a trumpet, and many of the Israelites came to him and joined his company. He sent messengers to others asking them to come and fight for Israel.

Gideon wanted God to show him whether or not he would win a battle against the Midianites. He put a fleece on the ground outside his house, saying that if, in the morning, there was dew on the fleece and it was dry on the surrounding ground, he would know that he would win the battle. When he got up to look, the fleece was wringing wet and the ground around it was dry.

Gideon advanced on the Midianites with only three hundred men. The Midianites, and their allies the Amalekites, were down below the Israelites in the valley. First of all Gideon went down on his own, as a spy, and was appalled to see his enemies as numerous as grasshoppers and accompanied by many camels and other animals.

He went back and divided his three hundred men into three companies, and he gave every man a trumpet, a pitcher and an unlit torch. They crept down the hillside after dark, and each man in each company simultaneously blew a terrific blast on his trumpet and smashed his pitcher. Then they shouted out, 'The sword of the Lord and of Gideon!' Total panic erupted in the enemy camp, which was entirely taken by surprise, and the people got up and fled. Lighting their torches, the Israelites burned their camp and pursued their enemies.

ABIMELECH

So long as Gideon was alive the Israelites remained faithful to God, but as soon as he died they turned back to worshipping the gods of Baal.

Gideon had fathered many sons. One of these was Abimelech. He wanted to be head of the family, and by appealing to many of his older relatives and persuading them to give him money, he almost achieved it. Then, by a trick, he got all his many brothers together in one place, where he and his followers turned on them and killed them.

One brother escaped by hiding. He was the youngest of Gideon's sons, and he was called Jotham. He cried out to the men of Shechem that they should avenge themselves on Abimelech, but instead of that they made Abimelech king. Abimelech had a reign full of violence and bloodshed. He died besieging a tower. A woman on the tower threw a millstone down on his head. He knew that it had mortally injured him, but rather than have it go down in history that a woman had killed him, he persuaded his armour-bearer to run him through with his sword. However, history still relates the story of the woman.

JEPHTHAH'S DAUGHTER

Jephthah was a great leader and warrior in Israel and he defended the Israelites against the Ammonites, who wanted to destroy them. One day, when he was about to go into battle against the Ammonites, he made a vow to God that whatever he first saw when he returned home he would offer as a sacrifice to God. His battle against the Ammonites was very successful – he put them to flight – and he went joyfully home. As he reached his house, his daughter and only child came out to meet him, singing and dancing. He tore his clothes in agony, and eventually told her about his vow. She replied to her father that he must, of course, fulfil his vow to God, since God had done such great things for the Israelites. All she asked was that she might be granted two months to go to the mountains with her friends to come to terms with what had happened. After two months she returned to meet her death. The young women of Israel held days of remembrance for Jephthah's daughter every year.

Samson kills the lion   The Philistines are killed   Judges 13-16   Delilah cuts Samson's hair and
delivers him back to the Philistines

Samson recovers his strength
and breaks the pillars

Ruth 1-4

Ruth, Naomi and Boaz

THE STORY OF SAMSON

The Israelites were in despair. The Philistines ruled over them, and their lot was hard. Then an angel appeared to an Israelite woman and told her that she would bear a very special child who would free Israel from the Philistines. He would belong to a sect of holy men called the Nazarites, who never cut their hair. Samson was born and grew up with long, thick hair.

To the distress of his parents, Samson fell in love with a Philistine woman and wanted to marry her. One day, on his way to visit her, he encountered a lion, which attacked him. With extraordinary strength, he killed it with his bare hands. The next time he passed that way he noticed that a swarm of bees had made their home inside the carcass. He took some of their honey and ate it, and took some home to his father and mother.

A wedding feast was arranged by Samson for his bride. Thirty young Philistines came to share the feast with him, as was the custom. Samson made a speech and told them that he had a riddle for them to solve in seven days. The prize was a suit of new clothes each.

'Go on then!' they said. 'Ask us your riddle!'

'From the one who ate,' Samson said, 'came forth food. From the strong came forth sweetness.'

After several days of struggling with this conundrum, the Philistine guests told Samson's wife that she must wheedle the answer from Samson or it would be the worse for her.

'I know you don't love me,' she told Samson, 'or you would share the riddle with me.' She wept and was offended for the whole seven days of the feast. At first Samson resisted, but in the end, in desperation, he told her. She went at once to the guests and told them the secret.

Gloating at his discomfiture, the Philistine men said, 'What is sweeter than honey, eh? What is stronger than a lion?'

Samson realised what had happened. He was furious. He went to Askelon, the Philistine capital, killed thirty men and gave their clothes to the guests at the feast. He gave his new wife away to a friend, and returned angrily to his father's house.

Months later he was still seething with rage against the Philistines, and determined to do them harm. He attached burning torches to the tails of foxes and set them to run through the Philistine corn. The corn was dry, and the fire quickly set the harvest alight and then spread to the vines and the olive trees. The whole harvest was ruined.

The Philistines hunted Samson, and he went into hiding. Some of the Israelites came to him and said that, since the Philistines ruled them, they felt Samson's actions placed them in terrible peril. They felt they had no choice but to deliver him to them.

They brought him, bound, into a Philistine town. Suddenly, however, a feeling of great strength came upon Samson. He broke the ropes on his arms as if they had been cotton, and then snatched up a bone lying by the roadside. Using it as a weapon, he killed many of his would-be attackers, so that soon he escaped them altogether.

When Samson got to Gaza he stayed in the house of a local woman. The citizens knew he was there and told themselves that when morning came they would kill him. But Samson got up at midnight, when the city was locked, and picking up the gates of the city, locks, bars, posts and all, carried them on his shoulders to the top of a local hill, where he threw them down.

Once again he fell in love with a Philistine, this time a woman called Delilah. The Philistines knew there was something uncanny about Samson's strength, and they asked Delilah to try to discover its source and whether there was a way they could defeat him. They promised to make her a wealthy woman if she betrayed his secret.

Delilah asked Samson why he was so strong and whether any sort of rope could possibly bind him. Samson kept giving false reasons.

Delilah begged and begged him to tell her the truth, as a sign of his love. Samson did love Delilah and wanted to believe that she loved him, too. Finally he told her the truth, which was that his strength came from the fact that his hair had never been cut, and that if it was cut his strength would leave him. Delilah sent secretly to the Philistine leaders while Samson was asleep. She had a servant cut off all his hair, so that when the Philistine soldiers arrived and she woke him, he no longer had the strength to resist them. The Philistines blinded Samson, bound him with brass chains and made him labour in their prison.

One day they gave a feast in their banqueting hall in honour of their god, Dagon. They invited all the noblest people in the city, and Samson was brought in chains from the prison and made to stand between the pillars in the centre of the hall where they could mock him. After a bit Samson asked the boy who had led him from the prison to help him to one of the pillars so that he could lean against it. The boy did so. Samson prayed to God that once again he might feel the return of his old strength. Then he held the two central pillars of the building, one in each hand.

'Let me die with the Philistines,' he prayed to God. He braced himself, and with an almighty effort pulled down the whole building upon himself and all the Philistines inside it.

RUTH AND NAOMI

Naomi lived in Moab, until suddenly her husband and her two sons died within a year of each other. Naomi was an Israelite, and she decided to return to her people in Canaan. Her two daughters-in-law, Orpah and Ruth, accompanied her. Orpah came part of the way and then returned to her people in Moab. Ruth, however, refused to leave Naomi.

'Do not ask me to abandon you,' she said. 'I love you and I want to stay with you always.'

The two women travelled on together until they arrived at Bethlehem at the time of harvest. To provide them both with food, Ruth joined the gleaners who picked up the corn from the ground after the reapers had cut and stacked the sheaves.

Boaz, a wealthy landowner, came to the field to see how the work was going, and met Ruth. He had already heard the story of her loyalty to her mother-in-law and had been moved by it, and after this he took particular care of her. He told her to be sure and help herself to water whenever she needed it, as well as the food he provided at midday. He secretly arranged that his men should drop corn from the sheaves in the fields where she worked so that she would find more of it. Ruth went home with plenty of corn and Naomi was delighted. She told her that Boaz was a relative of her dead husband.

Ruth continued to work in Boaz's fields till the end of the harvest. Naomi could see that Ruth liked Boaz very much. It was the custom for one of the men of a family to marry a widow so that she would not be left alone in the world, and Boaz was a near relative. Naomi suggested that Ruth should go boldly to Boaz and tell him that, in accordance with the custom, she would like him to marry her.

Boaz was delighted at her asking him. Unfortunately there was another family member who had first claim to Ruth, and unless he agreed Boaz could not marry her. Boaz went to talk to the relative, and as a result he negotiated to buy land that had belonged to Naomi's husband. It gave him the right to marry Ruth. They married, and Ruth bore a son who would one day be the grandfather of King David.

The image of Dagon is smashed

Baby Samuel
is presented to Eli

I Samuel 1-13

Samuel hears God's voice

Samuel finds Saul hiding

Samuel argues with Saul

Samuel anoints David

David slays Goliath

David escapes, helped by his wife

I Samuel 16-19

Saul tries to kill David while he is
playing the harp

THE CALLING OF SAMUEL

There was a good man called Elkanah, who lived in the hills of Ephraim. He had two wives, Peninnah and Hannah. Peninnah had many children and was always boasting about them. Hannah had no children and was very hurt by Peninnah's boasts. Elkanah, however, loved both his wives equally, and when Hannah cried about her lack of children and refused to eat because she was so unhappy, he would tell her how much he loved her. 'Am I not better than ten sons?' he would tease her.

One day the family went on a visit to the Temple. Hannah was feeling wretched because Peninnah had been unkind to her as usual, and she prayed with deep feeling. She made a vow to God that if he gave her a son she would bring him up a Nazarite, a man specially dedicated to God.

The priest, Eli, was sitting close to where Hannah was praying, and seeing her weeping and her mouth moving as she made the vow, he thought at first that she was drunk. He went to her and rebuked her for drinking.

'My lord,' Hannah said to him, 'I promise you I have not been drinking. I was asking God for help out of the fullness of my heart.'

Her reply convinced Eli, and he said, 'Go in peace. Whatever it was you asked God for with so much feeling, let him grant it to you.'

Elkanah and Hannah went back to their home in the mountains, and soon Hannah did conceive and bear a son, to her great joy. She called him Samuel. She weaned him lovingly and cared for him, and as soon as he was old enough she took him to see Eli.

'Do you remember me?' she asked him. 'I am the woman whom you thought was drunk, when I was standing here praying. God gave me a son, as I asked, and I am now giving him back to God as I promised to do. I want you to take my child and bring him up in the Temple.'

So Eli took the little boy and began to teach him the duties of the Temple. Every year after that, when Hannah and her husband came to the Temple to worship, Hannah would bring Samuel a little coat she had made for him. Eli blessed Elkanah and his wife, and prayed to God that Hannah would have more children to replace the one she had dedicated to God. She did in fact have five more children.

Eli had two grown-up sons of his own, Hophni and Phinehas, of whom he was not at all proud. They took advantage of their position as the sons of a priest to steal meat that people had given to the Temple for sacrifices, and they slept with the serving women of the Temple. It was a matter of great grief to Eli, but he could not stop them.

As Samuel began to grow up, Eli was growing blind and feeble. One night when he and Samuel were both in bed, the boy heard a voice, calling 'Samuel!'

He ran in to Eli and said, 'You called me?'

'I did not call you,' said Eli. 'Go back to bed, my son.'

Samuel went back to bed, and once again he heard a voice, calling 'Samuel!' Once again he ran in to Eli, and once again Eli insisted that he had not called him. It was very puzzling.

Then the voice called a third time, and this time it occurred to Eli that God must be calling the child.

'Go back to bed,' Eli said, 'and this time, if you hear the voice calling your name, I want you to reply. This time you will say, "Speak, Lord, for your servant is listening."'

The voice did call again: 'Samuel! Samuel!' and Samuel replied exactly as Eli had instructed him.

God told Samuel that he was going to destroy Eli's family because his sons had behaved so wickedly in the Temple and Eli had not stopped them. Samuel lay awake for the rest of the night, wondering what he was going to tell Eli.

In the morning, he got up and opened the doors of the Temple as usual. Eli sent for him, and, wise old man that he was, he could see at once what was wrong.

'Tell me everything that God said to you,' he said, 'and do not hide anything.'

So Samuel did so, and Eli only said, 'What God does is right in my eyes. Let him do what is just.'

Samuel grew up, and it was clear to everyone that he was going to become a great prophet – he was already famous for his wisdom.

It was a hard time for the Israelites. First they were defeated in battle by the Philistines, and many Israelites were killed. In order to give them courage they had the Ark of the Covenant brought into the camp – it was carried by Eli's two sons, Hophni and Phinehas. The Philistines attacked, killed Hophni and Phinehas and took the Ark of the Covenant, the most precious possession of the Israelites. When the messenger came back to Shiloh to tell the people what had happened, he came with earth smeared on his face and his clothes torn. The people gave a great shout of grief when they heard the story, and Eli, sitting on a seat by the gate of the city, heard it. He begged the messenger to tell him what had happened, and the messenger described the defeat of Israel's army, the death of Eli's sons and, finally, the loss of the Ark. When Eli heard of the loss of the Ark he fell backwards off the seat, which broke his neck and killed him.

The Philistines took the holy Ark and put it into the temple of their god, Dagon, at Askelon, as an insult to the Israelites. The next morning, when they went into the temple, they found the image of Dagon lying on its face on the ground. They put it back, but the next day it was the same. Again they put it back, but when they tried again to enter the temple, they found the head and the hands of Dagon lying on the threshold. Many people were suddenly taken ill, and they began to beg their leaders to get rid of the Ark before the whole country was destroyed. Eventually, the Philistine leaders became so frightened of the God of Israel that they returned the Ark with a gift of jewels inside it as a sign of their repentance.

Samuel, who was a grown man now, became the acknowledged leader of the Israelites. He told them that it was time to stop worshipping animals and strange gods, and to return wholeheartedly to the God of Israel. If they did so he would deliver them from the power of the Philistines. Samuel offered sacrifices to God on Israel's behalf. The Israelites did battle with the Philistines and took back all the towns they had occupied.

A KING FOR ISRAEL

For a long time the Israelites had wanted a king who would be able to rule over them when eventually Samuel grew old and died. Samuel tried to dissuade them, but they insisted, and at last God decided that they should have their king. It was to be Saul, a tall and handsome young man, the son of a wealthy and powerful man of the tribe of Benjamin.

Saul knew nothing of this. His father had sent him with a servant to look for some missing horses, but he and his servant rode for miles without being able to find them and eventually realised that they were lost. They realised that they were quite close to the city where the seer Samuel lived, so they decided to go in search of him, make him a gift of silver and ask him for help, both in finding the horses and in discovering their way back home. They were told that they would find Samuel offering a sacrifice at an altar in the city of Shiloh, so they went in search of him.

The previous day God had told Samuel that soon he would meet a young man from the house of Benjamin, and God would tell him when he did so. He must anoint him to be king over Israel, in order to free the people from the threat of the Philistines. As Saul came up to speak with Samuel, God said to him, 'Here is the man who will be king!'

Saul asked Samuel to tell him the way to the seer's house. Samuel said, 'I am the seer. Come with me to the altar and then you shall dine with me, and tomorrow you will go on your way after I have told you the secret of your life. Do not worry about the lost horses, by the way. They have been found. Now I have to tell you that the hope of Israel lies with you and with your father's house.'

Saul was baffled by this conversation. 'My tribe is the smallest one in Israel,' he said, 'and my family is nothing unusual.'

Samuel took Saul and his servant into the guest house of the holy place and made him sit in a place of honour among his guests, and he told the cook to give him the best portion of meat. Later he took him to his house in the city, where they sat together on the rooftop and talked. The next morning, when Samuel was bidding Saul goodbye, he sent the servant on ahead, saying that he had something private to say. Then he took a vial of oil, poured it upon Saul's head, kissed him, and told him that he was anointing him as king of Israel. Saul found it all very difficult to believe.

Samuel summoned all the people to a great gathering, with the idea of presenting Saul to them as their king. Saul took fright, and went and hid himself, but the people found him. Samuel stood him in front of all of them and said, 'Behold the one whom God has chosen!' And the people all shouted, 'God save the king!' Saul was taken to Gilgal and crowned king.

Saul was a powerful king. In the second year of his reign he and his son Jonathan began attacking the Philistines and winning victories over them, and they followed this with other victories over peoples who threatened them. But Saul was wilful and selfish and quarrelled with Samuel, and eventually God told Samuel that Saul could no longer serve Israel as king. Samuel grieved for Saul, because he loved him.

THE ANOINTING OF DAVID

One day God told Samuel to stop grieving and to go to see a man called Jesse who lived in Bethlehem. Jesse had many sons. One of them God had selected as the future king of Israel, and Samuel must go and anoint him. Samuel said that he did not dare, that if Saul found out he would kill him. God told him to go to Bethlehem on the pretext of offering a sacrifice, and to invite Jesse and his sons to attend.

Each of Jesse's six sons passed before Samuel, and as he saw each one he felt certain this was the one chosen, until God told him otherwise.

'Is this all your children?' Samuel finally asked Jesse.

'There is David, the youngest,' Jesse replied, 'but he is out in the fields looking after the sheep.'

'Fetch him!' said Samuel.

David hurried in from the fields. He was a beautiful boy with a ruddy complexion.

'This is the one!' God told Samuel. 'Anoint him.' So David became king, though no one knew it except his family. He went on living with his father and working in the fields.

Meanwhile Saul was suffering from moods of depression and anger. The only thing that seemed to help him was for a musician to play to him upon the harp, which he found soothing. Saul asked for such a man to be sent to him, and one of his servants remembered that David, Jesse's son, was a gifted musician, so they sent out into the fields to find David as he kept his father's sheep. Jesse was very flattered at the request and sent David to Saul with gifts of wine and bread and a kid. David played the harp for Saul, and Saul took a great liking to him. Every time one of Saul's bad moods came on, David would play to him and make him well. Saul liked him so much that he made him his armour-bearer.

A new crisis arose with the Philistines. The army of the Philistines and the army of the Israelites were drawn up close to one another waiting for the inevitable battle. One day a huge Philistine called Goliath strode out into the valley between the two armies. He was a giant among men, and he looked taller because of his huge helmet and his armour made of brass. He carried a staff as big as a beam. He shouted that he was the champion of the Philistines, and that if the Israelites wanted to fight they should send out a champion against him. If Goliath won, then the Israelites must be the slaves of the Philistines. If the Israelite champion won, then the Philistines would be the slaves of Israel.

The Israelites were appalled. None of them dared to go out and fight the Philistine champion, though day after day for forty days he stood in the valley and taunted them. The three eldest of Jesse's sons were with Saul, waiting to fight the Philistines. David, however, had gone home to help his father on the farm.

One day Jesse gave David bread to take to his brothers and a gift of cheese to the captain of their company, and told him to go and see how they were getting on. While David was talking with his brothers, Goliath came out as usual to challenge the Israelites. David was deeply shocked that Goliath should defy God, as it seemed to him. The soldiers told him that whoever killed Goliath should be made rich and should marry the king's daughter, but that did not interest David – he was only troubled about the insult to God. David suddenly announced that he was ready to fight Goliath, and news of this quickly reached Saul.

Saul sent for David, who repeated his willingness to fight Goliath. Saul told him that it was quite impossible, since he was only a boy and Goliath was a seasoned soldier. David then told him how, when he had been keeping his father's sheep, first a lion and then a bear had come to take lambs out of the flock, and how in each case he had killed them. God had been with him then, and he would be with him as he fought Goliath. Gradually he convinced Saul, and Saul finally gave him his blessing. At Saul's suggestion, David tried on his armour, but he soon realised it was too heavy for him. He took it all off again, and went to the brook and chose six smooth stones. He put them in his shepherd's bag looped over his shoulder, and he held his sling in one hand and his staff in the other.

When Goliath saw that his opponent was a mere boy he laughed scornfully. 'I'm a dog, am I, that you come to chase me away with a stick? Come here, boy, and I will give your flesh to the birds and the foxes.'

David replied, 'You come to me with sword and spear and shield, but I come to you in the name of the Lord of hosts, the God of the Israelites whom you have defied. Today you will die.'

Goliath came to meet David, and David ran to meet him, watched breathlessly by the Israelites. David put his hand in his bag, took a stone and propelled it with his sling. It struck Goliath on the forehead and entered his head, and immediately he pitched on to his face on the ground, dead! David ran, took up Goliath's own sword and cut off Goliath's head.

The Philistines rose in terror and fled, and after them flew the armies of the Israelites. David carried Goliath's head to Jerusalem, and when Abner, the general, took him before Saul, he presented it to the king.

I Samuel 20-28

Jonathan sends messages to David   David cuts Saul's robe   David and Abigail   The witch of Endor

II Samuel 1-18

David celebrates the return
of the Ark

David sees Bathsheba

David sends Uriah into battle

Absalom is caught by his hair

SAUL AND DAVID

aul was delighted at David's triumph over Goliath and he took him to live in his palace. He made him a senior officer in his army and gave him servants to wait on him. Saul's son Jonathan, a brave young soldier himself, took a great liking to David, and David returned Jonathan's regard. The two of them quickly became the closest of friends.

David's success had brought him instant fame throughout Israel. As he returned with Saul from pursuing the Philistines, women came out to greet them, singing, 'Saul has killed his thousands, but David his tens of thousands.' Saul was deeply offended by this, and sank into one of his black moods. He wondered if David might be plotting against him to take over the kingdom.

That night he invited David to come and play the harp for him, as he had so often done before. As David played, Saul's fear overwhelmed him, and he picked up a spear that was lying nearby and flung it at David to pin him to the wall and kill him. It missed him, but as David turned to flee Saul flung another spear at him. Again it missed. This suggested to Saul that God was on David's side, and he became even more afraid of him. He dared not publicly attack David, so he made him a captain over a thousand men, which took him away on duty.

David, deeply shocked by Saul's violence, said nothing about what had occurred but got quietly on with his new work. He was immensely popular throughout Israel. Saul pretended that he loved him still, and he suggested giving him one of his daughters as his wife. He

knew that his daughter Michal was very attracted to David. Saul instructed his servants to sound David out about marriage. They were to say that Saul loved David deeply and wanted to make him his son-in-law. Perhaps scenting a plot, because he now knew Saul was dangerous, David replied that he was not worthy to be the king's son-in-law; he was too poor, and of too humble a family. His words were duly reported back to Saul.

Saul did have a plot, of course. He now told the servants to say that if David and his men killed a hundred Philistine men and brought back their foreskins as evidence of what he had done, he would not hesitate to let David marry Michal. Saul's hope and belief was that, in carrying out this violent scheme, David would be killed himself and then would trouble him no longer. David was overjoyed, however, when he heard the news; he promptly acted on the suggestion and brought Saul the foreskins. Saul had no option but to let David marry Michal. It deepened his fear of David, however, and his mad belief that David was his deadly enemy. He became so obsessed by the idea that he told Jonathan and his servants that he wanted David killed. Jonathan was horrified, and at once told David of Saul's threat. He told him to go into hiding until he found out more about Saul's intention.

When Jonathan and Saul went out hunting together, Jonathan talked to him about David, saying that David was devoted to Saul, was innocent of any plot against him, and had done great service to Israel by killing Goliath. It would be a sin on Saul's part to shed the blood of an innocent man like David. Saul's fears abated as Jonathan talked, and he began to think he must be wrong. He swore to Jonathan that he would not kill David. Jonathan took David back to the palace to meet Saul, and things seemed to be normal between them, as in times past.

Soon there was another war against the Philistines, and once again David covered himself in glory. Because Saul was again in one of his moods when he returned, David played the harp to him. Again Saul threw a spear at him.

David fled and hurried back to his own house. Saul sent men after him to watch him, with orders to kill him in the morning. Michal saw the men, and guessed the meaning of it. She told David that if he did not escape at once, he would not live another day. She let him out of a window by a rope, and he fled to a hiding place. She put a statue in the bed to make it look as if someone slept there.

The next day Saul sent messengers asking for David, and Michal said, 'He is sick.' Then Saul came himself; he insisted on going to the bedside, and discovered what Michal had done.

'Why have you deceived me?' he asked her furiously. 'You have allowed my enemy to escape.'

Meanwhile David had escaped to Ramah, and had made his way to the old prophet Samuel, to whom he poured out the whole story. Saul's spies soon reported to him that David was staying with Samuel in Ramah, and Saul sent men to bring him back, eventually going there himself. He collapsed when he got there, stripping off all his clothes and lying naked on the floor babbling before Samuel for a day and a night.

David fled back to Jonathan, begging him to tell him what it was he had done to be hunted and threatened with death by Saul. 'There is,' said David, 'only a step between me and death.' Jonathan promised that he would do anything in his power to protect him.

'Very well!' said David. 'Tomorrow is the new moon, when I am invited with the other senior men for the three-day feast with the king. Instead of going to the feast I shall hide in the country, as I did before. If the king comments on my absence, tell him that I asked your leave to go home to Bethlehem for a religious ritual with my family. If the king says, "That is well," then we know that I am safe. If, however, he is very angry, then it will be a sign that harm is intended towards me.'

Jonathan said, 'God forbid that any harm should come to you – I know you have done no wrong. If I was sure that the king intended to harm you, I would tell you so. If he seems kindly towards you at the feast I will let you know. If it looks as if he means to harm you, I will tell you that, too, so that you can go away in peace, and may God be with you.'

The two of them swore an oath of friendship, so that, whatever Saul did next, they would always remain friends, close together in their love for God and each other.

'Go and hide in the field where you hid before for three days,' said Jonathan. 'On the third day I shall come into the field, near to where you are hiding, for shooting practice. I will shoot three arrows near to where you will be, and I will send a boy to fetch them. If you hear me say to the boy, "Please pick up the arrows," then you will know that it is safe for you to return. If, on the other hand, you hear me say, "Don't bother about the arrows. They are too far away for you to find," you will know that you must go away into hiding.'

On the first day of the feast Saul presided on his throne, with his general, Abner, on one side of him and the empty seat of David on the other. Saul did not ask after David. On the second day, however, he asked Jonathan why David had not appeared, and Jonathan explained that he had asked him for leave to go back to Bethlehem.

Saul immediately became maddened with rage and accused Jonathan of taking David's part instead of that of his own kin. He told him to go at once and fetch him, or he would have him killed.

Jonathan went out with a servant to the place where David was hiding and, as he had promised, issued a warning. Then he sent the boy home ahead of him carrying his weapons. David came out of hiding, and the two men wept together and again swore eternal friendship. David went back into hiding, and Jonathan returned to the city.

For many months David travelled from one country to another in fear of his life. For a while he lived in a cave at Adullam, where many men, some of them outlaws, came to join him. Saul was now suspicious of everyone, even his own followers, and he was determined to capture David and kill him. At one point he and his soldiers almost trapped David, but news of a Philistine attack called them away.

Another time David was in rocky desert country at En-gedi, and Saul pursued him there with three thousand men. Exhausted from his journey, Saul lay in the mouth of a cave and slept, not knowing that David and his men were already hiding in the cave. David's men urged him to kill Saul, but instead he cut off part of his robe. When Saul woke up and started to leave, David called after him, 'My lord the king!' and he bowed low before him.

David said, 'I could have killed you today, and my men urged me to do so, but I would not do it because you are the Lord's anointed. See, here is the skirt of your robe in my hand. Here is the evidence that I bear you no ill-will and have done nothing against you, and yet you hunt me down to kill me. I shall never harm you. May the Lord deliver me from death at your hand.'

Saul suddenly wept and said, 'Is this you, my son David? You have rewarded me good for evil. May God reward you for your goodness. Now I know that you will one day be king.'

On that occasion they parted almost as friends, but Saul soon began to distrust David again. The wars with the Philistines, and his own unhappiness, drove him to despair. He consulted a witch at Endor and asked her to call up the spirit of Samuel, the dead prophet. When Samuel appeared, Saul poured out his troubles to him and begged him to

comfort him, but Samuel could only tell him that David would soon be king and that he and all his sons would shortly be killed by the Philistines. This happened. Saul and Jonathan both died shortly afterwards in a great battle on Mount Gilboa.

Then the elders of Israel came to David in Hebron, and asked him to let them anoint him as their king. He was thirty years old and was to be the greatest of all Israel's kings, the one who was closest to God. He built himself a fine house of cedar in the fort of Zion, in the city of Jerusalem. He fetched the Ark of the Covenant, which had been hidden for safety in a house in Judah, and brought it up to Zion. There were great rejoicings as it entered the city of David, with music and people dancing and the crowds shouting. David himself danced with joy in front of the Ark. When the Ark arrived David offered sacrifices, and then he blessed all the people and gave every family a present of bread and wine and meat so that they might go home and have a feast.

Now that David was king there followed a time of peace. A new prophet, Nathan, had arisen in Israel, and Nathan and David communed about the things of God.

One day, however, when David was walking on the roof of his house, he saw a very beautiful woman bathing herself on a rooftop below him. He enquired from his servants who she was, and was told that she was called Bathsheba and was the wife of a soldier called Uriah. David sent for Bathsheba and had sex with her, and some time afterwards she sent a message to David telling him that she was pregnant by him. At this time the Israelites were engaged in battle with the Ammonites. David summoned Uriah and sent a letter by him to Joab, his general, telling him to place Uriah in the forefront of the fiercest battle, knowing very well that he would almost certainly be killed. Joab did this, and Uriah was killed, as David had expected. Bathsheba mourned over her dead husband. When the proper period of mourning was completed, David sent for her and made her his wife. Later she bore him a son. David already had many wives and mistresses, but from the moment he had seen Bathsheba he longed to make her his wife.

Nathan came to see David and began to tell him a story. 'Two men known to us have been living in this city. One is rich and the other poor. The rich man has uncounted numbers of flocks and herds of sheep and cattle. The poor man, until recently, only had one little lamb. His children loved it, and it was in and out of his house as if it was a dog. One day, not long ago, when the rich man wanted to hold a feast for a guest, instead of using one of his own sheep he stole the poor man's lamb, killed it, and had it cooked for his guest.'

David was shocked by this story, and urged Nathan to tell him who the rich man was.

'You are the man!' said Nathan. 'God gave you everything a human being could want, but you must have Uriah's wife too, and therefore Uriah had to die!'

David was deeply ashamed, and admitted to Nathan that he had sinned before God. Almost at once the son that Bathsheba had borne became ill. David fasted and lay all night upon the earth praying, but still the child died. This was the punishment for his wicked behaviour. Then David rose up, washed himself and put on clean clothes, to go into God's house and worship him and ask his forgiveness. Then he went to comfort Bathsheba. Later David and Bathsheba were to have another son, the great Solomon.

ABSALOM – THE REBELLIOUS SON

King David had many sons. One of them, Absalom, was one of the handsomest men in Israel, though he was also very conceited. He was not a loyal son to David, though David loved him dearly. One day Absalom hit on the idea of leading a rebellion against David in order to become king himself, which could not have hurt David more. Eventually, word came to David that Absalom intended to kill him, and David left his palace in Zion and fled to the country, where he quickly obtained a large following of fighting men.

Some of the leading men of Israel could not make up their minds whom to follow, David or Absalom. Ahitophel, David's own adviser, joined Absalom, while others remained staunchly loyal to David. One of those who remained loyal was Hushai, who asked David if he might go to Absalom as a spy and pretend to join his cause. This he did.

One day Absalom asked advice of Ahitophel and Hushai. Ahitophel advised Absalom to seek out David and to kill him alone, so that his followers would come over to Absalom. Hushai, however, advised Absalom to take on David and his men in battle (he knew what a large army David had assembled around him and what a brilliant general David was). Absalom chose the second alternative, which would be fatal.

Knowing what was coming, David grouped his men in companies for a tremendous battle, but he gave orders that Absalom was, if possible, to be spared. By chance, however, Absalom, who was riding a mule, rode under an oak tree, and was caught up in the branches by his long hair and left hanging there as the mule ran away. Some of David's followers, in spite of his instructions, thrust a spear through Absalom's heart as he hung, still alive, in the tree. Then they took him down and put him in a pit, and buried him with stones.

A messenger went to David and told him the good news that his men had won a great victory. David asked immediately, 'Is Absalom safe?' The messenger declined to answer, but another messenger then arrived and told him of Absalom's death. David went alone into his room and wept. 'O my son Absalom, my son, my son Absalom! Would that I myself had died in place of you, O Absalom, my dearest son!'

Solomon's judgment

I Kings 1-10

The building of the Temple

The Queen of Sheba arrives bearing gifts

THE REIGN OF KING SOLOMON

The time came when David grew old and frail and unable to rule his kingdom any more. An upstart called Adonijah tried to seize his throne and to persuade important men in Israel to follow him. David was determined that Bathsheba's son Solomon would follow him as king, but Nathan the prophet, knowing how feeble David had become, was afraid that everything would go wrong – Adonijah was plotting to kill Solomon and reign in his place. He went to see David and told him of the threat of Adonijah, and the old king roused himself and took action. He instructed Nathan to put Solomon on the royal mule and then to ride down with him and his servants to Gihon, where kings were crowned. There he and Zadok the priest must anoint Solomon king.

This took Adonijah completely by surprise. After Solomon was anointed there was a great noise of trumpets and pipes and singing, and the people all shouting, 'God save King Solomon!' Adonijah, sitting at table with his guests, heard it and said, 'What is that noise?' A visitor who had just arrived told him that Solomon had just been made king, so Adonijah knew his plot had been foiled.

Knowing that he was about to die, David instructed Solomon in the arts of kingship, and told him above all to worship God and to follow the law of Moses. They discussed which people a king needed to be lenient to, and which needed a stern hand.

One of Solomon's first actions after David's death was to form an alliance with Pharaoh of Egypt. He married his daughter and brought her back to live with him in his palace. He was trying very hard to be a good king and to be faithful to God. Once, after he had been praying, God appeared to him in a dream and asked him what he would like above all things. Solomon poured out his longing to be a good king who would measure up to his father David, but said that he felt too ignorant, too inexperienced, to carry the great responsibility of kingship. What he would like God to give him was wisdom – an 'understanding heart' which knew how to judge between right and wrong, good and bad.

God, who had expected him to ask for long life or riches or success in battle, was very pleased with this answer, and assured him that he would make him wise, and that he would also grant him the riches and honour he had not asked for. If Solomon continued to try to be faithful to him, like his father before him, then God would also grant him a long life.

Solomon awoke from this dream, and at once his wisdom was tested. Two women came before his judgment seat. They lived in the same house, they told him, and they had each given birth to a child within three days of one another. One baby died in the night, and its mother crept silently to the other woman and stole her baby, putting the dead one in its place. The woman who awoke and found the dead child beside her recognised that this one was not her child, however, and had come to Solomon to tell him of this terrible deed. The other woman insisted that the live child was hers.

Once Solomon had grasped all the details of the story he demanded that a sword should be brought to him. When it arrived he told his servants to cut the baby in half and give half to each woman. The woman who was the mother of the baby could not bear the thought of its being hurt and cried out at once, 'Give her the baby!' whereas the other woman was in favour of Solomon's suggestion. Solomon said that the woman who would rather give the baby away than let it be hurt must be the true mother, and he handed the baby to her. This story was repeated all over Israel as a sign of the king's wisdom and cleverness.

Israel was prosperous and at peace, almost for the first time in its history, and Solomon's reputation spread to other countries. He was admired and respected by other kings, who came to visit him and listen to his words.

Solomon remembered how King David had always longed to build a temple to God, but the continual wars and the poverty they brought had made it impossible to achieve. But now, in a period of prosperity, he knew that the time had come to start building. Hiram, king of Tyre, who had always admired King David, sent friendly messages to Solomon. Solomon, in reply, told him about his plans for the Temple, and asked him to send him timbers of cedar and fir from his lands with which to build. In turn Solomon would repay him with wheat and oil. Solomon sent his men to Lebanon to cut trees, and carry timber, and Hiram arranged for the timber to be floated down to Israel by sea.

Then the Israelites began to build the Temple. The design was very beautiful, with the floor and walls made of fine wood and stone. There was a special chamber for the Ark of the Covenant with huge cherubim carved out of olive wood to protect it. The inner walls were carved with flowers and palm trees, and the floors were covered in gold. All the sacred vessels were made of gold and silver and brass.

There was a splendid ceremony as the Ark of the Covenant, with the tablets of stone inside it, was carried by the priests into the Temple and placed in the special chamber. Suddenly the whole Temple was filled with smoke, as the glory of the Lord shone within it. Solomon offered and dedicated to God the house he had built for him. Then he turned round and blessed the people, and reminded them how David had longed for such a temple. Solomon prayed out loud, holding up his hands to heaven and saying, 'Lord God of Israel, there is no God like thee.'

He offered sacrifices, and then gave a feast for the people that lasted eight days. Soon he had another dream, similar to the one when God had promised him wisdom. This time God told him that he accepted the gift of the Temple, and would reside there with his people Israel for ever. He impressed upon Solomon how important it was that the people should remain faithful to their God, and not follow after idols or do wicked things.

Because the country was at peace, and because of his friendship with King Hiram and other monarchs, Solomon became exceedingly rich, and his palace and the kingdom itself were filled with beautiful objects that had come from far-off places. The Queen of Sheba, a woman of great wealth and discernment, heard so much of Solomon's wisdom, of his skill as a writer and thinker, and of the wonders of his country, that she came to visit him. She brought him many precious things – camels bearing spices, gold and precious stones – but what she had really come for was to talk to Solomon about spiritual things. She and the king talked of the things of God and of other subjects at great length together. She was deeply impressed by everything Solomon said, but equally impressed by the taste and splendour of his house and kingdom.

'I had heard such great things of you,' she told him, 'that I simply had to come and see for myself. But they did not tell me the half of it. Your wisdom and prosperity is beyond anything I could have imagined. Your people are very fortunate, and I bless your God who chose you to bring judgment and justice to the people whom he loved.'

She made Solomon many more presents of gold and spices and precious stones. He in turn gave her many presents, until she, still wondering, returned to her own country.

Elijah and Elisha

After Solomon, many different kings ruled over Israel, but most of them forgot about their duty to follow God's commandments and serve the people. Things went from bad to worse. The worst king of all was Ahab. He chose a wife, Jezebel, who was as wicked and cruel as himself. Ahab and Jezebel turned away from God and started worshipping the animal gods of Baal. Jezebel feasted the prophets of Baal at her own table, and gave orders for the prophets of God to be hunted down and killed. Unknown to her, the steward of the royal household, Obadiah, who was a good man, hid a hundred of the prophets in caves and secretly sent them food.

There was a holy man living in Gilead called Elijah. With great courage – since Ahab was a tyrant – Elijah went to see him and prophesied that because of his wrongdoing there would be a great drought. Then God warned Elijah to go into hiding. Elijah fled and hid in a lonely place near the brook Cherith. Every morning and evening God sent ravens to bring him bread and meat. Elijah drank water from the brook until the brook dried up from lack of rain and he became desperate. Then God told him to go to a place called Zarephath, where there was a widow who would take care of him. Elijah travelled to Zarephath, and at the gate of the city he met the widow herself, gathering sticks. He called out to her, asking for a little bread and some water in a jug, a kindness that it was usual to show to travellers if they asked for it.

The widow shook her head sadly and said, 'I would gladly give you food, but because of the drought I have not got enough to feed myself. All that I have left in my house is a handful of flour in a barrel and a little oil in a jar. When you arrived I was collecting sticks to make a fire to bake bread for myself and my son. That will be our last meal, and after that we will starve.'

Elijah said to her, 'It is well. Go in and make the bread as you said. Only before you shape a loaf for yourself and your son, make a little one for me. Believe me, you will have enough flour in your barrel, and oil in your jar, until the rains return.'

The widow felt that she could trust this stranger, and she did exactly as he told her to do. As he had promised, in the days that followed there was always enough flour in the barrel and oil in her jar. It was a wonderful thing. She invited Elijah to stay at her house, and there was enough food for him, too.

Suddenly, however, the widow's son fell ill, and within a few hours he appeared to be dead. The widow was beside herself with grief and said angrily to Elijah, 'Is this your doing? Did you come here because of some wrong I may have done, and then decide to punish me by killing my son?'

Elijah was aghast, but all he said was, 'Give me your son!' He picked up the boy in his arms and carried him up into the loft of the house and laid him upon the bed. He cried out in agony to God, saying, 'Why, oh why, did you bring this suffering to the woman who befriended me?' Then he stretched himself over the child three times, as if warming him, and cried out, 'O my God, let the child's soul return to his body, I beg you.' Slowly the child grew warm, his colour returned, and he sat up and spoke.

Elijah took the little boy by the hand and led him downstairs to his mother and said, 'You see? He is alive.' The woman was overjoyed and grateful and ashamed of herself all at once.

ELIJAH AND THE KING

After three years of drought and famine, God told Elijah that it was time for him to confront King Ahab. At the time, Ahab and Obadiah his steward were frantically searching the country to find grass to feed the king's horses and mules. As Obadiah searched, he met Elijah. He recognised him and prostrated himself before him, asking, 'You are the lord Elijah?'

Elijah said, 'I am. Go, tell the king Elijah is here!'

Obadiah was very distressed and said, 'If I tell the king that, it will be as good as a sentence of death for me. The king is a very angry man. I will tell you what I fear. I will tell Ahab that I have found you, but in the meantime the Spirit of God will have carried you to some other place, and I shall be a dead man. I have tried to be loyal to God – I hid the prophets at great risk to myself, as you know. But now you say, "Go and tell Ahab Elijah is here!" I daren't do it.'

'It's all right,' said Elijah. 'I promise that I will show myself to King Ahab today.'

Like the widow, Obadiah felt that Elijah was to be trusted, and fearful as he was he went to Ahab and told him that he had found Elijah. Ahab at once set off to meet him.

When he came face to face with Elijah he said furiously, 'Are you the one who disturbs the peace of Israel?'

To which Elijah boldly replied, 'It is not I who disturb the peace of Israel. It is you, and your family, who have broken God's commandments and started worshipping Baal.'

Ahab was not accustomed to being spoken to like that, but Elijah went on: 'Since you believe in the gods of Baal, let us have a contest. Gather together the children of Israel on Mount Carmel. Send for the four hundred and fifty prophets of Baal, whom Queen Jezebel delights to entertain. We shall see who wins, Baal or the Lord God of Israel.'

Astonished at Elijah's speech, and looking forward to seeing him crushed and defeated, Ahab gathered the children of Israel on Mount Carmel with all the prophets of Baal, just as Elijah had instructed.

Elijah turned to the people. 'Are you hesitating between Baal and the Lord God of Israel? I tell you that if Baal triumphs in what is about to happen then you may follow Baal. But if the Lord God of Israel triumphs, then you must follow him.'

No one replied.

Elijah said, 'I am here by myself, the one and only remaining prophet of the God of Israel. Baal has four hundred and fifty prophets. So let us see what happens next. Let Ahab provide us with two bullocks. Let the prophets of Baal choose whichever animal they prefer, cut it into pieces for sacrifice, build wood to make a fire, but set no light to the wood.

'Then let them call upon their gods to bring fire to their sacrifice. I will do the same thing, only calling upon the God of Israel, and we will see who wins. Whichever of us succeeds, let the people of Israel worship that God. Do you agree?'

The people said they agreed.

Then the prophets of Baal chose a bullock, prepared it for sacrifice, laid it upon the wood and began to call upon the name of Baal, saying, 'O Baal, hear us!' The people watched intently.

The prophets continued shouting the prayer to Baal from morning to noon, but nothing happened, even though they leaped upon the altar and bawled even louder. At noon Elijah mocked them and said, 'Maybe your god is having a nap? Or perhaps he is chatting to a friend, or out hunting, or away on a visit? Call louder!'

The prophets of Baal shouted themselves hoarse, and cut their arms with knives, which was one of their practices, until they were covered in blood, but still nothing happened. All day it was the same – no voice, no response and, of course, no fire.

Elijah decided his turn had come. 'Come closer!' he said to the children of Israel, and as they moved towards him he began to repair the altar of God, which had been broken on the orders of Jezebel. He took twelve stones, one for each of the tribes of Israel, and with them he built up the altar. Then he dug a trench around it, and put the wood in order, and cut up the bullock. Then he did something surprising. He commanded that the bullock and the wood should be drenched with water, and the trench around the altar should be filled with water. No one could imagine how the sacrifice could burn when it was dripping wet.

Finally, Elijah prayed, 'O Lord God, the God of Abraham, Isaac and Jacob, let it be known today that you are the God of Israel, that I am your servant, and that I am doing what you command. Hear me, O God, so that these people may know that you are God, and turn their hearts to you again.'

Then, suddenly, the fire came, and burst into a great blaze over the sacrifice, and burned up all the wood and licked up all the water in the trench. The people were overcome with awe, and they fell to the ground, praying to God and shouting, 'The Lord – he is God! The Lord – he is God!'

'Go and eat your supper!' Elijah said to Ahab, 'for the rains will come now.'

He returned to Mount Carmel and lay face down upon the ground. He said to his servant, 'Go and look towards the sea and tell me what is there. Go and look seven times.'

When the servant looked for the seventh time, he said, 'I can see, miles away, a tiny cloud no bigger than a man's hand.'

Elijah said, 'Go at once to Ahab and tell him to prepare his chariot and go home to Jezreel, for the rain is coming.' As he spoke, the heavens grew black with rain clouds, a tremendous wind sprang up, and there was a great downpour of rain.

Ahab went at great speed to Jezreel, where Jezebel was waiting for him, but Elijah himself went even faster and got there before him. Jezebel knew he was there and sent a messenger telling him that he would be dead before another day was out.

For the first time Elijah was frightened, and he went away into the wilderness near Beersheba with a heavy heart. He sat down under a juniper tree and prayed to God to let him die, he felt so afraid. After a while he fell asleep there under the tree, and in his sleep he felt an angel touch him softly and heard him say, 'Arise and eat!' Elijah sat up and looked around, and he saw a cake baking on the coals of a fire and a pitcher of water standing by. He ate and drank and lay down again. Then, strengthened by the food, he got up and walked on, until he came to Mount Horeb, and there he lived in a cave for forty days and forty nights.

It was then that he heard God saying to him, 'What are you doing there, Elijah?'

And Elijah said, 'I am in despair. I have tried to serve you, and to lead the children of Israel to serve you, but they have forsaken you and killed your prophets, and I am the only one left. Now they seek my life, and I am afraid.'

God said to him, 'Go, stand on the top of the mountain where I can see you,' and Elijah did so.

A dreadful hurricane sprang up that tore at the mountain and tumbled the rocks. This was followed by a great shaking of the ground in an earthquake. After the earthquake came a terrible fire. After the fire came a still small voice. Elijah did not recognise God in the hurricane or the earthquake or the fire, but when he heard the still small voice he knew that God was speaking to him. Elijah was so overwhelmed that he wrapped his mantle round his face and stood in the entrance of the cave, waiting for whatever was to come next. Then he heard the voice of God, saying, 'What are you doing there, Elijah?'

Elijah repeated what he had said before. God did not reply to that, but told him to go and anoint Jehu to be king of Israel after Ahab's death, and to find a young man called Elisha who would one day become prophet in Elijah's place. He reminded Elijah that, despite his fears, there were still many people in Israel who remained faithful to God.

Elijah took heart and went down to Damascus, and on the way he saw the young Elisha ploughing with a yoke of oxen. As he passed him Elijah threw his mantle over him and walked on. Elisha left the oxen and ran after Elijah, saying, 'I must go back to say goodbye to my mother and father, and then I will follow you.' He did so, and became Elijah's companion and helper for the rest of his life.

NABOTH'S VINEYARD

Meanwhile, Ahab and Jezebel continued in their wicked ways. There was a good man called Naboth who owned a vineyard right beside Ahab's palace at Jezreel. Ahab said to Naboth, 'I want you to give me your vineyard so that I can make it into a herb garden. I will pay you for it, if you wish, or give you another piece of land.'

But Naboth said that he would not give the king his family inheritance. Ahab was very angry, and he went home and lay down on his bed at the palace in a sulk, and refused to eat. Jezebel asked him why he was unhappy and why he was not eating, and he explained to her his disappointment over the vineyard of Naboth.

'Who is king of Israel?' Jezebel asked him, 'you or Naboth? Get up and eat your food and be merry. I promise you that you will have Naboth's vineyard.'

Secretly she arranged for Naboth to be wrongly accused as a blasphemer, so that pious men would take him out and stone him. And that is what happened. When Jezebel learned that Naboth was dead she sent Ahab to take possession of the vineyard.

Then God sent Elijah to Ahab to accuse him of killing Naboth and robbing him of his vineyard. When Ahab saw Elijah, he said, 'Have you found me, O enemy of mine?'

Elijah replied, 'Yes, I have found you, you worker of evil deeds. One day, where the dogs licked the blood of poor Naboth, they shall lick your blood.' For the first time Ahab became frightened, and he put on sackcloth and ashes and was humbled with fear.

He died soon after, in battle against the Syrians. He disguised himself in order not to be a target in the battle, and a soldier shot an arrow at random, which pierced between the joints of his armour and wounded him. Ahab sat helplessly in his chariot till sunset, his blood ebbing away until he died. He was taken back to Jezreel, and the dogs licked his blood from beneath the chariot, just as Elijah had prophesied.

ELIJAH'S CHARIOT

Elijah was growing old, and when he was about to die he asked the young Elisha what he would like from him as a gift.

'A double portion of your great spirit,' Elisha said.

'You ask a hard thing for yourself,' Elijah replied. 'If you see what happens when I am taken from you, your wish will come true.'

As they continued to walk and talk together, suddenly a chariot of fire appeared, with horses that ran between them. Before Elisha could speak, Elijah had been taken up to heaven in the chariot.

Elisha cried out, 'My father, my father, the chariot of Israel … the horses … the fire!'

As Elijah was taken up his mantle dropped from him, and it fell upon Elisha. He saw Elijah no more. The prophets, who watched all this from Jericho, said, 'The spirit of Elijah has fallen upon Elisha.' They came out to meet Elisha and bowed before him.

Nebuchadnezzar's golden statue

Shadrach, Meshach and Abednego survive the furnace

Daniel 1-6

MENE, MENE,
TEKEL, UPHARSIN

Belshazzar's feast and the
writing on the wall

DANIEL AND HIS FRIENDS

The Israelites were never again to experience the peace and prosperity they knew in the reign of Solomon. In the reign of Jehoiakim, a terrible thing happened. Nebuchadnezzar, the king of Babylon, came with his army and stormed Jerusalem. He captured Jehoiakim, stole some of the sacred vessels from the Temple, and took them away to the house of his gods. Many of the Israelites were taken away to Babylon, and had to serve the king there.

One of these was a man called Daniel. He was placed in the royal household under the command of the chief eunuch. The king provided food for his slaves, but Daniel was distressed that he was expected to eat food that was forbidden to an Israelite. He suggested that the Israelites should be given only water and pulses for ten days, and at the end of ten days their appearance should be compared to that of other slaves, who ate meat and drank wine provided by the king. At the end of ten days they seemed in better condition than all the other slaves.

Daniel and his three friends, Shadrach, Meshach and Abednego, were noted for their knowledge and wisdom and their skill in interpreting dreams. Eventually Nebuchadnezzar learned of this and invited them to an audience. He soon found them much more helpful than the magicians and astrologers he usually employed.

One day he dreamed a dream so frightening that he woke in a cold sweat. Unfortunately he could not remember the dream, though he knew it was important. He sent for his magicians, and told them that they must tell him what he had dreamed and then interpret the dream, or he would kill them. They replied nervously that if he would tell them the dream they would be glad to interpret it for him. No man on earth, they said, could guess another's dream, or interpret it without being told what it was. The king flew into a rage and told Arioch, the captain of his guard, that all the wise men in Babylon must be killed.

When Daniel learned of this he said that he thought he could give the king the interpretation, but he needed a little time. He discussed it with his friends and they prayed about it, and in the night the secret was revealed to Daniel in a dream. Daniel awoke, full of praises for God, and he went at once to see Arioch and told him not to kill the wise men, as he knew the interpretation of Nebuchadnezzar's dream. Arioch hurried with Daniel to the palace.

'Can you tell me the content of my dream that I have forgotten, and then make known the interpretation to me?' Nebuchadnezzar asked Daniel sternly.

'No wise man on earth could do that,' Daniel replied, 'but the God in heaven who knows all secrets can do so, and he has revealed the secret to me – the secret of what shall happen in the days to come.

'What you saw in your dream, great king, was a huge statue of terrifying aspect. Its head was made of fine gold, its breast and arms of silver, and the belly and thighs of brass. These all shone brilliantly. The legs of the statue were made of iron, and its feet were made partly of iron and partly of clay. As you watched, a rock struck the feet of clay. It smashed them and down fell the whole statue, the gold and the silver and the brass and the iron, and broke into small pieces on the ground. Meanwhile, the rock that had broken the statue grew and grew until it was the size of a great mountain that filled the whole earth.

'This was your dream, O king. Now I will tell you its meaning.

'You are a great prince, a king of kings. God has given you power, strength and glory. You are the ruler of innumerable peoples, vast flocks and herds, countless lands. You are that head of gold that you saw upon the statue. After your reign there will be another kingdom not as great as yours – this will be the kingdom of silver. The next will be the kingdom of brass, and so on until the fifth kingdom, of clay, which shall disintegrate. When that time comes, God will institute another kingdom that will last for ever – this is the rock that will grow until it fills the whole earth. Your dream, and my interpretation, tell the truth about what is to come.'

Nebuchadnezzar was amazed at Daniel's words, and he bowed before him and offered him gifts. 'Your God,' he said, 'is a great God of gods, and a Lord of kings, since he could reveal to you this secret.' Nebuchadnezzar made Daniel ruler of the province of Babylon and chief of his wise men. At Daniel's request, his friends Shadrach, Meshach and Abednego helped rule Babylon.

Things went well for them until Nebuchadnezzar decided to have a great statue of gold made and set it up in Babylon. He commanded all the leaders of the people – princes, governors, captains, judges, treasurers, sheriffs and rulers of the provinces – to come to the dedication ceremony. When they stood in front of the statue, a herald announced that soon they would hear a burst of music – trumpets, flutes, harps, sackbuts, psalteries and dulcimers – and when they did so they must fall on their faces on the ground and worship Nebuchadnezzar's golden image. If they did not humble themselves before the king's power in this way, they would be thrown into a furnace and burned to death.

Of course, this put Daniel and his friends in an impossible position. They could not worship a false god, and yet not to do so was to invite certain death. When everyone else bowed down before the golden image, they quietly stayed away. This was noticed by others, courtiers already jealous of the power Daniel and his friends wielded in Babylon. They could not wait to go to the king and tell tales.

'You remember, O king, your decree that everyone must worship the golden image or else be thrown into the burning fiery furnace? We think you would wish to know that some of the Israelites, including some very powerful men, have not done as you commanded, and have not bowed before the golden image. These men are Shadrach, Meshach and Abednego.'

Nebuchadnezzar was very angry, just as the courtiers had hoped he would be, and he commanded that the men should be brought before him.

'Is it true,' he asked the three of them, 'that you did not bow down before the golden statue when you heard the sound of the music? Then you have one more chance. If, next time you hear the music, you bow down before the statue, I will forgive you, but if not, you will be thrown into the furnace.'

Shadrach, Meshach and Abednego answered very politely that they could not worship the golden image or Nebuchadnezzar's gods. There was no question about it.

Nebuchadnezzar flew into one of his terrible rages. He commanded that the furnace should be heated to seven times its usual heat, and that his soldiers should bind the three men and fling them into the furnace. The furnace was by then so hot that the flames killed the men who opened it, and others had to pick the prisoners up and throw them bound into the fire.

Nebuchadnezzar watched, and then, to his astonishment, realised that he could see not three but four men, all walking unharmed in the heart of the fire. The fourth man looked like a young god. At that, Nebuchadnezzar ordered Shadrach, Meshach and Abednego to come out of the fire, and they came out unharmed. He immediately made a decree that in future they should be required to worship no god but their own.

THE DOWNFALL OF NEBUCHADNEZZAR

Nebuchadnezzar believed himself to be the greatest king on earth. The only thing that troubled him was bad dreams. One night he had a dream that frightened him, and he recounted it to Daniel.

'There was a huge tree,' he said, 'the top of which seemed to reach up into the sky, and the roots down into the earth. It was beautiful, with shining leaves and many fruits. Birds fed from it and nested in its branches, and many wild animals liked to rest in its shade.

'Suddenly an angel appeared and commanded that the tree be cut down, that its branches be hacked off and the leaves and fruit allowed to wither. The birds and the animals abandoned it. All that was left was the stump rooted in the field. It was moistened by dew and rain, and was as low and humble as the beasts of the field. It would remain like this for seven years.

'None of my wise men,' said Nebuchadnezzar to Daniel, 'can make anything of this dream. But because the spirit of God is in you, I know that you will be able to tell me what it means.'

Daniel was astonished at what he heard, and was silent and troubled for a whole hour. Seeing his distress, the king said to him, 'Please do not let my dream disturb you.'

Daniel replied, 'My lord, I would like to think that the dream was about your enemies and not about you, but it is not so. The glorious tree that you saw, with its branches reaching up into heaven and the creatures nesting in its branches and sheltering beneath it, was yourself. Its greatness is your greatness. But the words of the angel describe what will happen to you, that you will be forced away from human habitation, and will eat grass like the wild animals, and live in the open where the dew will fall upon you. All this will go on for seven years as a result of your pride in your greatness. If, at the end of seven years, you recognise that your greatness is nothing as compared to the greatness of God, then your kingdom will be restored to you – this is the meaning of the stump still rooted in the earth. My counsel to you, O king, is to start to live a righteous life and show mercy to the poor, so that perhaps you may avert this tragedy.'

Nebuchadnezzar was very shocked at this saying, but the months went by and he remained as powerful as ever. He was congratulating himself one day on the splendour of Babylon and the glory of his own majesty, when suddenly he heard a voice from heaven saying, 'Your kingdom is departed from you.'

All at once Nebuchadnezzar became mad. He roamed out into the fields, eating grass like an animal, sleeping in the open, far away from the splendid life of the court and the civilising society of men. His nails grew long like claws, his hair was wild and unkempt, his body was burned by sun and soaked by rain, and he crawled on all fours like an animal.

After seven years his reason returned to him, just as Daniel had said it would, and he lifted up his eyes to heaven and praised the great God, and recognised his own nothingness compared to God. He went back to Babylon, and his throne was restored to him. He was a better king than he had been before because he was no longer vain and proud.

BELSHAZZAR'S FEAST

Nebuchadnezzar was succeeded as king by his son, who was called Belshazzar. He was an extravagant and foolish king. One day Belshazzar decided to give a feast. He invited a thousand of the nobility, and provided splendid food and wine. He had the sacred golden vessels of the Israelites, which Nebuchadnezzar had stolen from the Temple, brought to the banqueting-hall, so that the princes and his wives and mistresses could drink out of them. They all got very drunk and spoke praises of the idols that they worshipped.

Suddenly something terrifying happened. A huge hand appeared and began to write on the wall opposite to where the king was sitting. He went pale and began to shake. He could not read the writing, so he sent at once for wise men, saying that whoever should read these words and explain them should be given rich clothing and a chain of gold, and should hold high office in the kingdom. But none of the wise men who came could make sense of the writing on the wall.

Seeing his distress, his queen reminded him how much his father had been helped by Daniel, and how clever he was at interpretations of dreams and explanations of spiritual matters. So Daniel was sent for.

Belshazzar told him what good things he had heard about him, and the presents he would give him if he could read the writing on the wall. Daniel said that he had no need of gifts, but that he would read the writing.

'The writing on the wall,' Daniel told Belshazzar, 'said, "Mene, Mene, Tekel, Upharsin".' It was a warning from God that the Chaldean kingdom was finished, that Belshazzar had failed as king, and that the kingdom would fall into the hands of the Medes and Persians. That night the kingdom was overrun by Darius the Persian, and Belshazzar was killed.

DANIEL AND THE LIONS

When Darius began to rule over the Chaldean kingdom, he made Daniel the chief overseer. This was much resented by his subordinates. They plotted his downfall, but could find no grounds for disgracing him since he was a faithful servant to King Darius. With great cunning, however, they went to Darius and suggested that he should make a decree that, for thirty days after his reign began, no one should pray to any god or make a petition to anyone, except Darius himself. If anyone defied this decree they should be thrown into the den of lions as a punishment. The decree was very flattering to

Darius, and he signed it. The Medes and Persians had a strict rule about royal decrees, that once they were drawn up and signed by the king there could be no going back on them, even by the king himself.

Unaware of the danger that he was in, Daniel went into his house and, with his windows open facing Jerusalem, he knelt and prayed out loud to the God of Israel as he had always done. Those who plotted against him stood outside his house and listened to him, and then went to the king and told him that Daniel had defied his decree.

Darius was very distressed and ashamed of himself when he heard this, because he deeply respected Daniel. He did everything he could think of to try to save him. His courtiers, however, pointed out that no decree or statute signed by the king could be changed – that was the law of the Medes and Persians. So the king was obliged to condemn Daniel to death.

When Daniel was brought in, the king talked with him in private, saying that he prayed his God would deliver him. Daniel was thrown into the lions' den, a stone was rolled across its mouth and cemented into place, and the king stamped the seal with the royal signet ring, as was the custom. He spent the night awake and fasting. He got up very early in the morning and went to the lions' den, and cried out piteously, 'Daniel, O Daniel, you who serve the living God, has your God saved you?'

Daniel called back, 'O king, live for ever, I am alive and unhurt. God sent his angel to keep me.' The king was overjoyed, and commanded that Daniel be lifted out of the den. He sent for the courtiers who had accused Daniel and had them thrown to the lions, and he issued a decree throughout his realm that Daniel's God was indeed the living God.

Esther and Mordecai
outwit Haman

Esther 1–10

Jonah sets sail in the storm

QUEEN ESTHER

Jonah 1-4

Jonah is swallowed by the
huge fish

Jonah is miserable as God
destroys his gourd

QUEEN ESTHER

Ahasuerus, the king of the Medes and Persians, was very angry. He was one of the mightiest kings on earth, who reigned over a vast empire and owned untold wealth. When he gave a feast to his princes and nobility in the palace of Shushan, the guests reclined on beds of gold and silver on floors of coloured marble, and drank exquisite royal wine out of gold cups.

The king had a desire to show his queen, Vashti, a very beautiful woman, to his guests, and he sent an order that she was to come to him, wearing her royal crown and robes. To his horror, she sent back a message that she would not come. Since he had sent for her very publicly, it made the king look foolish and hurt his pride, both as man and as emperor. He was giving a party to show that he was the richest and most powerful man on earth, and his own wife disobeyed him! His advisers told him that he must act firmly (they were afraid, they said, that their own wives might start imitating Vashti's disobedience), and under their influence Ahasuerus decided he had had enough of Vashti and her whims. He would look for a new wife.

Accordingly he ordered that, in all the provinces of his kingdom, suitable young women should be collected together and brought to Shushan, and out of them all Ahasuerus would choose a new queen.

As it happened there was an Israelite called Mordecai who lived in the palace. He was one of those who had been taken captive by Nebuchadnezzar and forced to leave his own country. Mordecai had a cousin called Esther, an orphan whom he had brought up and cared for as his own child, who was young and beautiful.

Mordecai suggested to Esther that she might join the young women from whom Ahasuerus was about to choose a wife, and he took her to see Hegai, the king's chamberlain, who had charge of the women in the palace. Hegai took a liking to Esther and resolved to try to help her. At Mordecai's suggestion Esther said nothing to anyone about the fact that she was an Israelite. Like all the women, Esther had to undergo a long purification process before she was allowed to meet the king, with her body being anointed with precious oils. She became a great favourite with everyone in the house of women, while Mordecai watched from afar to make sure that she came to no harm.

Ahasuerus saw each of the women who had been sent to him, one by one. After they had had their interview they returned to a different house, and remained there in case the king wished to see them again. Only those who were specially favoured were asked back for a second visit.

Esther was as great a success with the king as she had been with everyone else at the palace, and he decided that she was the one whom he wanted as his queen. He had her crowned in Vashti's place, and gave a great feast to mark the occasion.

By chance, while Mordecai was idling in the courts of the palace trying to get a glimpse of Esther, he overheard a conversation between two doormen of the palace, who were plotting to kill the king. When he next saw Esther he told her about this, and urged her to tell the king as quickly as possible. The matter was investigated and it turned out to be true.

About this time Ahasuerus appointed a courtier called Haman to be his right-hand man. All the nobles bowed to him, as did everyone else, but it was noted that Mordecai did not bow when Haman passed. Some of the king's servants, currying favour with Haman, told Haman how Mordecai did not bow and suggested that it was because he was an Israelite, something Haman had not known.

Haman was very angry at what he thought of as Mordecai's disrespect, but instead of simply punishing him he took it into his head to punish all the Israelites in the kingdom.

'My lord,' he said to Ahasuerus, 'there is throughout your kingdom a people who are different from all other people, and who hold the king's laws in contempt. I want your permission to get rid of them. I don't mind paying those who kill them myself so that your majesty is not out of pocket.'

The king took off his seal ring and gave it to Haman, so that he could write to all the provinces of the empire saying that any Israelites, old or young, who lived in them must be killed. Haman did this, and he sealed his letters with the king's seal.

All the Israelites were aghast when they heard the terrible news, and they began to weep and pray and fast, and beg God to deliver them.

Mordecai dressed in sackcloth and went and sat in front of the king's gate. (No one was allowed to go into the courtyards of the palace wearing sackcloth.) Esther, who did not know about the decree to kill the Israelites, saw her cousin there and was embarrassed, so she sent him proper clothes to wear. When he sent back a refusal, Esther asked a chamberlain called Hatach to find out the reason for his distress. Mordecai told him about the decree for the destruction of the Israelites, and of how Haman had himself paid money to bring it about. He gave him a copy of the decree to show to Esther, and he asked him to beg her to go before the king and plead with him for her people.

Esther sent back a message to Mordecai that it was strictly forbidden for anyone, including herself, to go in to see the king unless he summoned them himself. He had not summoned her for thirty days. The punishment for going uninvited was death, though if the king felt kindly he could hold out his golden sceptre, which meant that he wished to see the visitor.

Mordecai's reply to this message of Esther's was that she was no more likely to escape death than any other Israelite, so she had little to lose by braving Ahasuerus. Silence could be fatal. Perhaps, however, God had made her the queen for just this reason – to save her people from destruction.

Back came Esther's reply: 'Gather together all the Israelites you can find, and all of you fast from food and drink for three days and nights and pray for me. I too will fast for three days and nights, and so will my maidservants. After that, I will go in to the king, and if I perish, I perish.' It was a brave response.

On the third day, after her fast, Esther dressed herself in her royal robes and went to stand in the inner court of the king's house where he could see her. He saw her and held out the golden sceptre.

'What do you ask of me, Queen Esther?' he enquired affectionately, and then joked, 'Whatever you request you may have, up to half of my kingdom.'

'My lord, I would like to give a banquet today, and I would wish that you and Haman would attend it,' Esther replied. The king agreed at once, and ordered Haman to come.

As they sat at table the king said again, 'What is it that you ask of me?'

'Tomorrow I shall hold another banquet,' Esther replied. 'I want you to come once again with Haman. Then I shall tell you my request.'

Haman was very pleased at these marks of royal favour, and went home and told his wife about his growing success and the riches he was accumulating. The only thing that spoiled it for him, he said, was the sight of Mordecai at the king's gate, refusing to bow or stand up or even show that he had noticed him at all.

'Don't let that trouble you,' said Zeresh, his wife. 'Go out now and order a gallows to be built, and tomorrow ask the permission of the king to hang Mordecai upon it!'

THE FALL OF HAMAN

By chance the king could not sleep that night, and he asked for a record book to be brought to him to while away the hours. As he read, he came across the incident of the men who had conspired to kill him, and the account of how Mordecai had prevented it.

'What honour has Mordecai received as a result of this?' he asked his servants, and they said, 'No honour, my lord.'

Next morning Haman stood in the court waiting to ask the king for permission to hang Mordecai on his gallows, and the king invited him in.

'What should be done for a man whom the king delights to honour?' Ahasuerus asked. Haman secretly thought the king meant himself, but he did not show it and replied, 'He should be dressed in the king's clothes, and set on the king's horse and led through the city by one of our great men, who will call out, "This is a man in whom the king delighteth."'

'Good,' said the king. 'Then take the clothes and the horse just as you described to Mordecai the Israelite, and you yourself can lead him through the streets and sing out his praises, for he has done us great service.'

Haman was mortified, but he had no choice but to obey the king. As soon as he had done the king's bidding, he hurried home in grief, and poured out his troubles to his wife, Zeresh.

'If Mordecai is an Israelite,' Zeresh said shrewdly, 'and you have begun a persecution of the Israelites, then things look black for you.'

As they talked, the king's chamberlain came to conduct Haman to Queen Esther's banquet. While they sipped their wine Ahasuerus again questioned Esther. 'What is your wish, my queen? It is my pleasure to grant it.'

'O king,' said Esther, 'I am asking you for the favour of my own life and that of my people. For the decree has gone forth that we are to be killed, every one. If it had simply been that we were to be sold into slavery, I would have held my tongue, but I cannot be silent when so many are to die.'

Ahasuerus did not know what she was talking about. 'Who is he, where is he, that would think of killing my beloved queen and those dear to her?' he asked.

'He is here. It is Haman, who has sent out to all your provinces a decree that the Israelites must be slaughtered. And I myself am an Israelite.'

The king was so angry that he got up abruptly from the banquet and went out into the palace garden to control himself. Haman saw the king's anger, and used his absence to beg Esther to grant him his life. He threw himself on his knees by her couch, begging and beseeching. The king returned and ordered Haman to get away from his wife, and that he should be placed under arrest. One of the servants mentioned that Haman had recently built a gallows on which to hang Mordecai, and the king ordered that Haman should be hanged on his own gallows.

Esther, however, could think of nothing but the terrible decree that condemned men, women and children to death throughout all the king's provinces. It might even now be being carried out. She begged the king to act quickly, to send letters reversing the decree by camel and fast horses all over the kingdom so that her people would be saved. The letters went out immediately, sealed with the king's seal.

Meanwhile Mordecai was given splendid clothes by the king, a sumptuous garment of blue and white, with a purple coat of fine linen and a golden crown.

As word of their deliverance spread all over the provinces of Persia, the Israelites began to rejoice and feast and celebrate their happiness.

Ever since that time, their descendants, the Jews, have remembered that wonderful day and the courage of Queen Esther, and have held a feast they call Purim. On it they give one another presents, and give alms to the poor.

JONAH AND THE WHALE

Jonah was a prophet. One day God told him to go to the great city of Nineveh and preach a sermon there, rebuking the people for their wickedness. Jonah was terrified at the idea – the people would probably kill him – and, trying to escape from God, he went to Joppa and boarded a ship going to Tarshish. It was about as far from Nineveh as he could get.

Once the ship was at sea a storm blew up, with fierce winds and huge waves. So bad was it that even the experienced sailors on the ship felt it was hopeless, and they began praying desperately to their gods.

Jonah had gone below decks and did not wake during the commotion. The captain kicked him and said, 'How can you lie there asleep? Wake up and pray to your God to save us.'

The sailors thought that their peril might be due to there being someone on the ship who was bringing them bad luck. The way to find out was to draw lots. The lot fell upon Jonah.

'What have you done to bring this trouble upon us?' the sailors asked him. 'Who are you, and where do you come from?'

Jonah told them how he was an Israelite, and explained how his God had told him to do something which he had refused to do. 'Fling me into the sea!' he said bravely. 'I think this tempest is my fault.'

They did not want to do this and rowed as hard as they could to try to bring the ship to land, but it was impossible. So they threw Jonah into the sea as he had advised them, and at once the water became calm, which made them feel a great respect for Jonah's God.

Jonah sank down deep into the water, with seaweed wrapping itself around him, and he naturally assumed he was going to drown. Instead, he was swallowed up by a huge fish and went down into its belly, where he lay terrified for three days and three nights. There he prayed in agony to God, begging for some deliverance from his living hell, and he promised that if God saved him he would serve him better in future. To his astonishment and joy, the fish then vomited him out on to dry land.

Once again God gave Jonah the order to go to Nineveh, three days' journey away, and this time Jonah went immediately. He began to preach, saying that in forty days, because of the wrongdoing of the people, the city of Nineveh would be overthrown. To Jonah's surprise, everyone listened to him. The king of Nineveh, learning of Jonah's mission, proclaimed a strict fast and the wearing of sackcloth, and told all the people that they must turn from violence and try to be better people.

His hope was that God might give them another chance.

That was exactly what happened. When God saw how hard they were trying he decided not to destroy Nineveh. Jonah was not pleased at all, perhaps because it made him look foolish. What he had prophesied had not come to pass. 'Was it for this,' he asked God, 'that I have suffered so much?'

He went off in a sulk and made a little shelter for himself with branches, where he could watch the city and see whether the prophecy might still come true. It got very hot under the shelter, but God made a gourd plant spring up to protect Jonah from the sun's heat, which was a great relief. But the next day the gourd was eaten up by a maggot, and Jonah fainted in the unbearable heat of the sun's rays. When he recovered, he begged God to let him die, he was so miserable.

'You are angry about the death of the gourd?' said God. 'Do you not think I would find it painful to see the destruction of the many thousands of people in Nineveh, people whom I created? Show a little mercy towards them, and you will feel better.'

THE TESTING OF JOB

There was once a very good man called Job. He loved God and was kind to his neighbours. He was rich, and owned many sheep and camels and oxen and horses. Because of his wealth and his noble character, he was shown much respect. He also had a wife who loved him, and ten fine children.

By chance, he became the subject of a conversation between God and Satan (the devil). Satan had come to see God, as he sometimes did, and God asked him where he had been and what he had been doing.

'Going to and fro in the earth, and walking up and down in it,' Satan replied.

'In that case,' said God, 'I hope you noticed my servant Job. He is a man of the greatest goodness. He must be a great disappointment to you, who like to tempt men and women into doing bad things.'

'On the contrary,' replied Satan, 'I can see well enough why Job is a good man. You have given him every advantage a person could have – wealth, possessions, family, good health and a happy life. Who wouldn't be good with all that to enjoy? But just you try taking some of that away from him and see what happens. He would soon curse you.'

Satan's words angered God, and he said, 'Very well. Let us test Job. You may take his advantages from him, only do not destroy him.' So Satan set to work.

There came a day when Job's children were happily eating together in the house of the eldest son. His oxen were ploughing in the fields, with the horses quietly grazing in the nearby fields. His sheep were in the fold with their shepherds watching nearby.

Suddenly a message came that some brigands called the Sabeans had come and stolen the oxen and the horses, killing the herdsmen who tended them. Only one of the men had survived to report the disaster. Job was shocked, but before he could recover another messenger arrived to say that all Job's sheep had been burned up in a fire, and the shepherds with them. Only one shepherd had escaped in order to tell the news.

Finally, and much more terribly, word came that while Job's sons and daughters were eating and drinking together, a hurricane had sprung up and had caused the roof to fall in on them all, and only one child remained.

Job was broken at the horror of it all. He tore his clothes and shaved his head, and fell down upon the ground in his grief. But he worshipped God, saying, 'Naked came I into the world, and naked shall I go out of it. The Lord gave, and now the Lord has taken what he gave away. Blessed be the name of the Lord.'

Satan came again before God, and when God asked him where he had been and what he had been doing, he replied as before, 'Going to and fro in the earth, and walking up and down in it.' As before, God asked Satan if he had noticed the perfection of Job. Although Satan had caused Job to suffer extremely, yet still he held fast to his faith in God.

'That's all very well,' said Satan. 'Possessions and family are important, but what finally influences a man is his own well-being. If you attack Job's own person, you will find it is a very different story.'

'All right!' said God. 'You may try the

experiment again, only you must preserve Job's life.'

Satan went away, and he afflicted Job with painful boils all over his body, which were sore and also itched so much that he could only get relief by continually scratching himself with a bit of broken pottery. No one could have felt more wretched, and he was in utter misery.

His wife was indignant on his behalf, and told him to forget his devotion to God. 'Curse him and die!' was her advice. Job rebuked her for her words and said, 'We received much good at the hand of God, did we not? We were very fortunate. Should we not also be prepared to receive hardship and suffering?'

Job had friends called Eliphaz, Bildad, Zophar and Elihu, and when they heard of his terrible distress they decided they must come and try to comfort him. They were very shocked when they saw him – his suffering had changed him so much.

Then Job broke down. He cursed the day he was born, and told his friends that he would rather die than live in his present torment. He found it almost impossible to sleep, but when he did sleep he had terrifying dreams. He hated his sick body and could see no point in his life at all.

His friends tried to say helpful things, but they did not really listen to him. They told him that maybe his suffering was his own fault, and that in any case he had no right to question what was happening to him. Job became angry at their superiority – it was easy to feel you knew all the answers when life was still going well with you. He did trust God in a way, but he wanted some explanations, and he did not feel that it was unreasonable of him to ask God for this. What had happened to him made no sense to him.

The friends continued to argue with Job and to sound more and more self-satisfied, until he decided he had had enough. He sent them away, calling them 'miserable comforters'. With their easy answers they had made him feel worse.

But what next? Job felt himself utterly alone, confronting and questioning God. It was at this moment that God, as impatient as Job himself with the small-minded friends, spoke to him.

'Listen, Job,' he said. 'I know what would help you most is to understand what is going on. Some of it you can understand. Some of it is too difficult for you, because you are a man, and I am God. I made the world, the sea, the earth, I designed day and night. I made the sun and the rain, the snow and the hail, frost and ice. I set the great planets in the heavens. I am the Lord of thunder and lightning, of the great lions and of the wild animals. I am the maker of a bird's wing and master of the powerful horse, of the whale, the hippopotamus and the mighty crocodile. I understand life and death. You will never be able to make sense of all that, and I cannot explain it to you. But trust me, Job. Get up, and begin your life again, and I will restore to you what you have lost. I love you still, and I commend your faithfulness, which is great. Never mind your friends. You are a good man, and I know it.'

Hearing God's words of love made Job wonder how he could have doubted him for a moment – as, of course, he had. But he was glad that he had challenged God about his suffering, because he felt as if he had now truly seen God and understood a little of his glory for the first time. He felt both repentant and very joyful, for God had answered him and restored his sense of dignity to him.

Meanwhile God rebuked Job's friends and told them to ask Job to pray for them, since throughout his ordeal he had remained a good man. God then restored his former wealth to Job, and gave him more children and possessions than he had had before. Job lived in good health to a great old age.

THE RETURN FROM EXILE

It was more than a hundred and fifty years since Nebuchadnezzar had besieged Jerusalem and carried many of the Israelites away to be slaves in Babylon. Since then Jerusalem itself had been almost destroyed, and more captives had been taken away to live in exile. They never ceased to long for their own country and for the great Temple of Solomon which stood in the midst of the city.

Many of the captive Israelites had risen to important positions under their masters – first the Chaldeans, then the Medes and Persians. One such man was Nehemiah, who was the cup-bearer (a sort of butler) for King Artaxerxes of the Persians, who valued him greatly. Nehemiah always longed to have news from Jerusalem, and one day a traveller supplied it. The people living now in Jerusalem were in a desperate state, he told him. Most of them were very poor and had a great struggle to live at all, since they were afflicted by drought and famine. Apart from the Temple, Jerusalem itself was largely destroyed, some parts of it by fire, some as a result of deliberate destruction by the attackers.

Nehemiah was devastated by the news. He wept and could not eat, and he prayed ceaselessly to God, mourning the wrongdoing of the Israelites which had brought about their downfall. They had deserved their fate, Nehemiah thought, but he begged God to remember his devotion to his special people and to find a way to help them.

One day, when Nehemiah was serving wine to the king, the king asked him what was the matter. He did not appear to be ill, the king went on, but why was he so sad?

Nehemiah was very frightened of offending the king, but he said bravely, 'O king, live for ever, how can I not be sad when the holy city of my people is in ruins? The city itself and the graves of my ancestors are laid waste, and the gates of Jerusalem have been burned down.'

'Are you asking me for help?' the king replied, to Nehemiah's astonishment. 'If so, what is your request?'

Nehemiah prayed quickly to God and then said, 'Would you allow me to go to Jerusalem, to the city of my fathers, and rebuild it?'

It was a very daring thing to say, but the king did not seem surprised. He and the queen looked kindly at Nehemiah and asked how long it would take him to get there and how long he was likely to be gone, and Nehemiah made a guess at the time it would all take. Then, since he had the king's ear, he asked for letters of safe-conduct to the governors in the countries he would need to pass through. The king agreed to this, and in addition suggested sending soldiers and horsemen along with Nehemiah.

More daringly still, Nehemiah then asked if the king might write a letter to Asaph, the keeper of the royal forest, asking him to supply timber to start the repairs in Jerusalem. The king, who had got interested in the project, cheerfully agreed to this too, and then appointed Nehemiah as governor of Jerusalem. Nehemiah felt that his prayers had been well and truly answered.

What Nehemiah did not know was that there was a handful of corrupt men, led by Sanballat, who was not an Israelite, who were making a living out of the sufferings of the poor in Jerusalem. They were not at all pleased when rumour reached them that a man was on his way to investigate the plight of the Israelites.

Nehemiah came quietly to Jerusalem and found himself somewhere to live. By night he and some friends went out on horseback to look at the walls and buildings, and everywhere they found devastation – walls smashed, gates gone, streets impassable because of rubble. The next day Nehemiah went to the Israelite community and told them that it was time to start rebuilding, to restore their beloved Jerusalem. He explained about his prayers and the effect they had had on King Artaxerxes. His audience were immediately captured by his vision and energy, and they announced their readiness to start work on the huge project.

As soon as word leaked out they were sneered at by Sanballat and his friends, who knew they would lose their livelihoods if the Israelites succeeded.

Nehemiah was a brilliant organiser. He had inspired many willing volunteers, some of them priests and educated men, some of them labourers. He divided them into groups and gave each group a particular responsibility, to replace gates or to strengthen the walls, often in the part of the city where they lived. The first thing the inhabitants needed was security from raiders and enemies, but after Nehemiah had talked to them they were also excited at the idea of restoring their great city to the beauty it had once known.

To begin with, Sanballat and his friends laughed at this workforce of amateur builders, some of them people who had never worked with their hands before. They sneered that the wall would be so badly built that even a passing fox would dislodge the stones. But then they suddenly realised that at least half of the walls of Jerusalem were now repaired and that the workers had made a very good job of them, and they stopped laughing. They decided to bring gangs of soldiers from outside to make a surprise attack all along the wall and kill those who opposed them.

Nehemiah secretly discovered this, and he set a watch along the wall and prayed to God for help. He armed each family with swords and spears and with bows and arrows, and stationed some men high up where they could shoot with advantage and others in secret places where they could suddenly ambush the enemy. News travelled to their enemies that Nehemiah and his men were ready for them, and they gave up the plan.

While the work was going on, Nehemiah discovered why some of the Israelites were so desperately poor. Because of the famine, they had been obliged to mortgage their houses and lands in order to buy corn, but the richer Israelites, who supplied it, were charging an enormous rate of interest which kept their fellow countrymen in perpetual poverty.

Nehemiah was very angry when he learned this, and he went to the rich Israelites and confronted them, and told them that they must restore to the people the ownership of their mortgaged lands and houses and cease ill-treating them like this in future. Such was Nehemiah's authority that they were deeply ashamed and took a solemn vow to restore all the property.

Finally the wall was finished, and all the gates were set in place so that it was possible to make Jerusalem secure at night and to watch who went in and out of it by day. The Israelites gathered together in the biggest street in the city, and Ezra the scribe stood up in a pulpit and read to them from the book of the law of Moses. The people were so moved to be listening to the law read in their newly restored city that they wept. Nehemiah, however, told them that it was a day for rejoicing, and that they should go home and feast with their families.

The singers and musicians rehearsed their music for the great day when the wall was to be dedicated. Half the people walked one way round the walls, and half the other way, while the trumpet sounded. The courage and determination of Nehemiah and the hard work of the people had restored their city to them, and they were overjoyed.